Soul Lanterns

UZKI

E JAPANESE

TRIERI

Soul Lanterns

DELACORTE PRESS

Translation copyright © 2021 by Penguin Random House LLC
Hikari no utsushie Hiroshima Hiroshima Hiroshima text copyright © 2013 by Shaw Kuzki
Jacket art copyright © 2021 by Shoko Ishida

Delacorte Press is a registered trademark and the colophon is a trademark of Penguin Random House LLC.

Visit us on the Web! rhcbooks.com

Educators and librarians, for a variety of teaching tools, visit us at RHTeachersLibrarians.com

Library of Congress Cataloging-in-Publication Data is available upon request.
ISBN 978-0-593-17434-0 (trade) — ISBN 978-0-593-17435-7 (lib. bdg.) — ISBN 978-0-593-17436-4 (ebook)

The text of this book is set in 13.25-point Adobe Garamond Pro.
Interior design by Carol Ly

Printed in the United States of America
10 9 8 7 6 5 4 3
First American Edition

For all the Hitomi Koyamas
in the world

Contents

Prologue

When the sunlight fades on August 6, the lantern floating begins by the bridge.

Lantern upon lantern of red and green paper.

Once their flames are lit, they begin to glow as if they're alive.

When you set them in the river, they shine their light on the dark water as well.

The lanterns and souls roll along together.

The lights gleam.

The lanterns pitch feebly, jostling together as they float away.

Some lanterns don't manage to join the current. They bob endlessly by the riverbank.

An old man in an open-collared shirt prods them with a pole.

Some lanterns tip over. They continue floating away on their sides.

The many-colored lanterns, their lights flickering, float away to the far-off sea.

Ever since she was too young to understand, Nozomi would see the lanterns off each summer with her family, and she would draw a picture in her journal for school. Her little brother, Akiyuki, would say the lanterns floating on the river looked like red and green cubes of *kanten,* and Nozomi, for her part, would recall an illustration from the story of Aladdin and thought they looked like the jewels he finds in the cave. Then she would bring her forehead right up to the paper and draw "The Night of the Lantern Floating Ceremony."

In the twenty-fifth summer since the bomb fell, Nozomi's mother knelt next to her and her brother in prayer. There were two lanterns floating away from her hands. The green one had a name written on it, but the white one did not.

That summer, when Nozomi was a sixth grader, she thought it strange for the first time. Last year and the year before, and probably the years before that, too, her mother had released two lanterns. A green one and a white one. The white one never had a name. Nozomi had always seen it off without thinking, but now she wondered: *Who is that lantern for?*

Nozomi's grandmother had also just gently released two lanterns. Each bore the name of a daughter. The pair of lanterns for the girls born a year apart glided onto the water's surface side by side as if holding hands. Their lights flickered, illuminating Nozomi's praying grandmother's profile and creating shadows in her deep wrinkles.

On the riverbank were about as many people as there were lanterns. There were even more people behind them. People were floating lanterns on the opposite bank, too.

Nozomi could see an old couple standing huddled together as they watched. Seven lanterns had just been released. Six were pale red, some almost pink, and just one, in the middle, like the center of a flower, was yellow.

The seven lanterns floated on the water like a fallen peach blossom and drifted away.

Following the blossom came another red lantern.

Nozomi felt like she had seen the person watching it somewhere before. But their face melted into the darkness, and the lantern joined the current and was swept away.

As Nozomi strained her eyes to look at the river's surface, someone was watching her intently. The gaze was so strong that she noticed and turned around.

The woman was about Nozomi's grandmother's age. When their eyes met, the woman's widened, and she stared at Nozomi even harder. Then she seemed to make up her mind and came over to her. "How old are you?" she asked.

1

The Strange Question

The way the old woman asked so pointedly, Nozomi didn't even hesitate before answering.

"I'm twelve."

The old woman shook her head and murmured something under her breath.

It sounded like "That can't be. . . ."

Nozomi felt shy for no real reason and lowered her eyes. When she saw the woman's worn-out shoes, she somehow felt like she had said something wrong. She looked away from her feet and added, "But I only just turned."

After remaining silent for a moment, the woman asked, her face tense, "Do you have an elder sister?"

When Nozomi shook her head and answered that she only had a younger brother, the woman looked disappointed. Then she started to walk away, but turned on her heel and came back.

The clinging look in the old woman's eyes frightened Nozomi, but she was rooted to the spot.

"How old is your mother?"

"She's forty-two."

Upon hearing her reply, the woman took a hard look at Nozomi's face. Suddenly, there were tears forming in her eyes.

Nozomi was startled, and the old woman apologized repeatedly, "I'm sorry, I'm sorry," as she fairly fled into the darkness.

Dumbfounded, Nozomi watched her go.

On their way home, Nozomi's grandma was walking with some friends from the neighborhood. Her mother, walking a few paces behind them, seemed to be pondering something.

Nozomi's mother had a more or less sunny personality, but when she was alone, she tended to read books and lose herself in thought. When Nozomi was little, she often felt, *Mommy's not here right now.* She would get impatient and whine. Now that she was older, she was capable of giving her mother some space when her mind was elsewhere, but this time she couldn't help but start a conversation. The shock of her interaction with the old woman still hadn't worn off.

"Ah, that was freaky."

"What happened?" her mother inquired absent-mindedly.

When Nozomi told her about the strange old woman, she stopped in her tracks. Nozomi stopped, too.

"And then she asked me, 'Do you have an elder sister? How old is your mother?'"

"How old is your mother?" her mother simply repeated, but she set off walking again at a quick clip.

Hurrying to catch up to her, Nozomi commented jokingly, "I must look like someone she knows. Or maybe you do?"

Everyone said she looked just like her mother, but Nozomi wondered if that was really true. Her mother's face was slender, while hers was round.

Whenever she mentioned that, though, her mother

would reply, "I had chubby cheeks when I was your age," and smile.

But now, instead of smiling, she said in a quiet voice, "There are still so many people looking for someone in Hiroshima."

That was true. Nozomi sometimes saw a man catching up to someone and grabbing their arm or a woman peering into the face of every person who passed by.

The morning of the atomic bomb, more than seventy thousand people were lost in an instant. Nozomi and her friends learned in their peace studies class that those people truly just "vanished." The temperature at ground zero rose to over seven thousand degrees, boiling blood and melting flesh. One person's shadow was even burned into stone steps.

Still, listening to her teacher, reading testimonies, seeing pictures, and visiting the Peace Memorial Museum, Nozomi had a hard time believing that something like that had really happened. Could people really vanish in an instant? Leaving behind only a shadow? It was difficult to imagine.

Surely everyone felt that way. Which was why so

many people couldn't believe their loved ones were gone and continued looking for them to this day. They clung to the idea that their family members, sweethearts, and friends had survived and were still out there somewhere.

"That old lady must have been looking for someone, too," said Nozomi.

"Someone who looks a lot like you."

"But it happened twenty-five years ago, ri—" Midquestion, Nozomi noticed her mother's face. She looked awfully pale, even though it was the kind of summer night that made you sweaty standing still.

Could it be that that lady was looking for her missing daughter, and it's my mom? She grew up, got married, and had a kid who looks just like Mom. Maybe that's why she asked how old she was. . . . And now my mom realized that and is wondering what to do . . . ?

Nozomi pictured Gramma, her grandmother on her mother's side.

Maybe Gramma adopted Mom, and Mom's real mom is this lady?

Nozomi loved stories, so when she read *Alone in the*

World or *The Prince and the Pauper,* she often amused herself by imagining that she was really a kidnapped princess or the daughter of a rich family with no obnoxious little brother. She had never imagined her mother in any of those scenarios, but once she started daydreaming, she felt like it almost sort of made sense.

No way. It can't be.

"I'm going ahead," she told her mother, and raced on as fast as she could to clear the old woman's tense expression—and the daydream, which was strange even for her—out of her head. Akiyuki took off right after her.

It was after Nozomi and Akiyuki arrived home that their mother and grandma got back. They went straight to the family altar, made an offering of incense, and prayed. Nozomi and Akiyuki sat quietly in a respectful posture behind them.

When it was Akiyuki's turn to offer incense, Nozomi was relieved to hear their mother chide him, "Don't blow it out. Use your hand to fan it." Maybe her pale face earlier had only been in Nozomi's head.

Since the beginning of August, a flame had burned

continuously at the altar. It was a sign to guide the returning spirits.

The altar contained the spirit tablets of all the people who were supposed to come back: their grandpa, their dad's two younger sisters, and one more—their dad's previous wife.

Their dad had made it back from a concentration camp years after the war ended and married again, this time to their mother, and then Nozomi and Akiyuki were born.

The lanterns their grandma had released bore the names of her two daughters: Yoshiko and Kyoko. They had both still been just students. They'd fallen victim to the bomb while they were out demolishing buildings as part of the student mobilization.

The green lantern their mother had released bore the name of their dad's former wife, Kumiko.

The house was about a mile and a half from the blast, but both Kumiko and their grandma had been thrown off their feet as they were working out in the fields. They both got burned from the waist down. Later they learned that it was because the black parts of their work pants absorbed the light. Some people even got burns in the shapes of the patterns on their clothes.

An acquaintance brought Yoshiko and Kyoko, who were badly burned, home in his truck. Though Nozomi's grandma and Kumiko weren't feeling well themselves, they went without sleep to care for the girls. When both daughters drew their last breaths one after the other, Nozomi's grandma became bedridden.

Kumiko pulled the dead sisters' bodies on an old cart to the place where people were being cremated.

After that, Kumiko continued looking after her mother-in-law and managing the household, but she grew weaker and weaker, and one morning at the end of the summer, she was found cold.

She must have thought she could still work. Nozomi had heard that her apron was folded neatly near her pillow, and in its pocket was a little scrap of paper. She had written a list of all the things she needed to do around the house, and of the five, only the first was crossed off.

She had been raised to be sophisticated and was talented in the flower-arranging art of ikebana, but she promised her husband, Satoru, when he went to war that she would "look after the home front," and she bravely faced any challenges that came her way. She hadn't even turned twenty yet.

In the picture of Kumiko on display in the altar room, she looked like a slender, delicate child. Nozomi had a hard time imagining her pulling a cart laden with two dead people.

Kumiko's name had been written on the green lantern. But the other lantern Nozomi's mother released, the white one, didn't have a name.

I wonder who that lantern was for. . . .

As Nozomi offered incense at the altar, the white lantern came to mind. She thought maybe it was for someone who wasn't represented on the family altar.

It happened later that day. The night was breezeless and muggy. When Nozomi woke up to go to the bathroom, she noticed a ray of light spilling from the door to the altar room.

She thought maybe the votive lights had just been left on, but when she peeked through the gap in the sliding screen door, her mother was sitting alone before the altar. Nozomi was about to call out to her when she realized with a start that her mother was softly crying. There was a small paper package in her hands, but by the votive lights alone, Nozomi couldn't tell what it was.

She looked at her mother's face again. She was still looking down at the package and crying when she abruptly turned to face a different direction. There was an ornate rosewood cabinet to the left of the altar, and she opened one of its drawers, put the package in there, and quietly closed it again. Then she turned back to the altar and brought her hands together.

Nozomi tiptoed away and went back to her room.

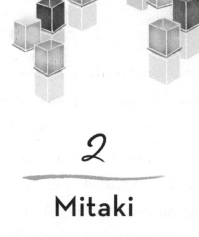

2

Mitaki

From above, the city of Hiroshima looks like an unfolded fan, and six rivers flow through it as if they were the fan's ribs. That geographical feature is known as a delta. It's beautiful to look at, but it also makes a great bombing target—that's what Nozomi learned in elementary school.

Of the six rivers, the biggest, which flows through the Chūgoku Mountains, is the Ōta River. Nozomi and Akiyuki had been going there to play since they were little, but they were always told, "Don't go in the water. The current will sweep your legs out from under you."

When you look from around Uchikoshichō to the big hill in Mitaki on the opposite bank, there's an area that looks like terraced fields. They were carved into the hill after the war to make a cemetery there. The gravestones are arranged neatly in rows, but it's not just their size and shape that are identical. Strangely enough, the inscriptions all have something in common. The year carved on the stone is always Shōwa 20—1945—the month is always August, and the date is almost always the sixth.

Nozomi had come to that realization around the same time she'd started to wonder about the white lantern. That was the previous summer, when she was in sixth grade.

One sunny spring Sunday, not so long after she started middle school, Nozomi was going to the cemetery with her mother and grandma. Her grandma hadn't been feeling well since the beginning of the year and had missed the opportunity to go during the equinoctial week, the traditional time for visiting ancestors' graves. She had been fretting about it ever since then and insisted on going.

Right as they were about to leave, Akiyuki said he would go along, too, so the whole family besides their dad would be there. Their dad worked for a car company and was stationed in New Zealand. Nozomi knew Akiyuki was only after the sweets at the Mitaki tea house, which would surely follow the grave visit, but their grandma was happy to have the family going all together.

As usual, they took a taxi up the road that led to the top of the terraced cemetery. After they got out of the car, Nozomi took her grandma's hand to steady her, and they descended the steps to the graves on the middle terrace.

Akiyuki went with their mother to fetch water. He was still little, and so bursting with energy that he ran everywhere. Usually by the time he reached the grave, his pail would only be half full. He always had to make a few trips, and Nozomi could hear their mother scolding him already.

As Nozomi and her grandma proceeded slowly down the hill, Nozomi saw someone who must have just finished a visit going down the lower path. He was looking down and limping, but walking at a quick pace.

Nozomi gasped. "That's one of my teachers!"

Her grandma looked surprised. "From the middle school?"

"Yes, the art teacher."

The man dragging his leg was definitely Mr. Yoshioka. Nozomi was in the art club, and he was the supervisor. Mr. Yoshioka had hurt his leg in the war, Nozomi had heard.

"So that's him . . . ," said her grandma.

Now it was Nozomi's turn to look surprised. "You know him, Grandma?"

Nozomi's grandma glanced at her. She seemed to be wondering if the story was something she could tell a child, or if Nozomi should even be considered a child anymore.

"He was engaged to Satoko Kikkawa." She gestured quietly to the next grave over. It was a plot for the Kikkawa family. In addition to incense, there were offerings of yellow chrysanthemums and paper-wrapped sweets.

Grandma said the Kikkawas lived in the same neighborhood as her family, but she hadn't realized they had neighboring grave plots, too, until they bumped into each other during a visit once. After all, it was a cemetery built after the war, and the names Kikkawa and Ota, Nozomi's family name, were both very common in Hiroshima.

"Even if you visit quite regularly, you don't often meet people here," Grandma said, looking toward the path Mr. Yoshioka had descended.

When Nozomi asked if she should go after him, her grandma shook her head. "When you go to visit the dead, sometimes you don't want to meet the living."

Despite the fact that she didn't entirely understand, the words felt heavy in Nozomi's chest.

"Did the bomb—the Flash—get the lady he was supposed to marry?"

Her grandma nodded.

Her mother had begun tidying up the area around the graves. Her grandma arranged the flowers, lit incense, and carefully poured water over the gravestones. Nozomi also took a turn pouring the water.

"You mustn't pour it over the top," her grandma warned her, as always.

Her grandpa had had thin hair, and while he was alive, when they went to the cemetery, he apparently always rubbed his head and said, "If you pour from the top of the stone, I'll be so cold. When I die, don't pour any near the top."

In the picture in the altar room her grandpa had such

a serious expression that whenever Nozomi heard that story, whenever she was pouring water over his grave, she wanted to burst out laughing.

Her grandpa died when she was just a baby, so she only knew him through photographs and everyone's stories of him. There were other funny stories, too. He used to say, "If I accidentally come back to life while I'm being cremated, I'll be so hot! Have the wake for two nights." The family honored this wish as well and held the wake in the altar room for two nights. "Luckily it was during a cold season," her grandma still said sometimes.

After praying over him for a long time, Nozomi's grandma spoke in the direction of the gravestones, as usual. She wanted Nozomi and Akiyuki to hear.

"Kumiko, you'll be happy to know Satoru is working hard. He's in New Zealand now. Yoshiko, Kyoko, your niece, Nozomi, has started middle school. Akiyuki is a second grader now. Please watch over both of them so they grow up safe and sound."

She turned around to look at Nozomi.

"Yoshiko was your age, and Kyoko was a year younger."

The sisters' names were carved side by side on the

gravestone. The date of death was Shōwa 20, or August 6. When they died they were fourteen and thirteen.

Nozomi was born in the summer, so she was still twelve. Her grandmother counted using the old age system. The previous year she had said, "Yoshiko was one year older than you, and Kyoko was your age." Once she had also said, "They say to keep counting the years of children who are gone, but I can't forget the way they looked when they left the house that morning."

Sometimes she seemed to be looking at Nozomi and yet not looking at her. She was remembering her dead daughters through her. Inside Nozomi's grandma, Yoshiko and Kyoko didn't age. They would always be first- and second-year students at the girls' school.

Will Grandma say the same thing again next year? wondered Nozomi. According to her grandma's way of counting, by then she would be older than her aunts would have been. Yoshiko and Kyoko would remain young girls, but Nozomi would grow up safely under her deceased relatives' care? She thought about those things as she prayed.

Akiyuki prayed after Nozomi, a meek expression on his face.

After offering the several white chrysanthemums she had set aside for the Kikkawa grave, their grandma prayed.

"You two should pray, too."

The incense Mr. Yoshioka must have offered was still burning.

"Poor Satoko. They never found her bones."

"Then what's in the grave?"

"I heard they buried a comb."

"A comb?"

"That was all they could find."

Her grandma stood and tucked away her jade prayer beads.

"The one who found the comb was the man who was here a moment ago."

Nozomi turned around to look at the path, although there hadn't been anyone walking down it for some time.

3

Mr. Yoshioka

*N*ozomi had Mr. Yoshioka for her elective art class, and he also supervised the art club, so she had had personal conversations with him before, but she couldn't bring herself to tell him she had seen him at Mitaki Cemetery.

He was old enough to be the students' father, but he looked much younger. Tan skin, a mop of hair. Gray smock, imitation leather sandals on his feet. Practically barefoot. When there were assemblies or ceremonies, he would show up in a beat-up suit and what looked like leather dress shoes. He was very thin, so whatever he wore was too big around his neck. And he never looked comfortable in his seat. Apparently he had a hard time with events like this, anything too showy.

One morning, Nozomi had been surprised to find his picture in the paper. He had won a prize at a big art exhibition. Not only that, it was the third time. When the principal mentioned it at the morning address and encouraged everyone to give him a round of applause, Mr. Yoshioka shrank in his seat, looking even more uncomfortable than usual.

He was a bit shy, maybe, but the look in his eyes was usually cheerful, and he never put down a student's work. If he didn't admire a piece, he just stayed quiet. He wasn't a big talker, but sometimes he joked about his legs—because he had a bad left leg and a limp. The story Nozomi and the other first years had been told was that he had been thrown overboard in the South Seas and a shark bit off his toes. The second years had heard they'd been bitten off by a Sumatran tiger he'd been playing with at the zoo. But they could see his toes in his sandals, and his left foot still had them, just like his right.

Mr. Yoshioka's eyes were bright, and he would tell tall tales in a dead-serious tone of voice, so Nozomi thought maybe Mr. Yoshioka wasn't the man in her grandma's story, that maybe it wasn't Mr. Yoshioka they had seen at the cemetery.

When art club ended and the members went home, Mr. Yoshioka always stood in the window of the art room in the old school building and saw them all off. The building had escaped the fires. The schoolyard and the pool had shielded it. Mr. Yoshioka would stand there all alone and watch the gate. When Nozomi and the others waved, he would wave back at them without fail, his arm tracing a big arc. They were too far away to really see his expression, but because his white teeth stood out from his dark, healthy skin, they could tell he was smiling.

First year Shun Nakamura had once borrowed an American magazine from Mr. Yoshioka, and he'd opened it to show everyone. "Look, he's just like this toothpaste ad." The man smiling with all his teeth showing in the American toothpaste ad had a thick jaw and a magnificent physique that made it clear he was getting proper nutrition. His chest seemed about four times thicker than their teacher's.

Everyone had turned to look at Mr. Yoshioka. He

was sketching the schoolyard. Focused on his drawing, he hadn't heard the cluster of students oohing around the magazine.

Nozomi had a feeling that the neck poking out of his smock had gotten even more spindly, so without thinking, she had said, "Just his teeth, though. His teeth are exactly like that, but nothing else."

She expected that Shun would have a comeback, but he just looked at Mr. Yoshioka in silence.

June was rainy, and at its end, the kids had self-study art classes twice in a row. That week, Mr. Yoshioka wasn't around for art club, either.

"Mr. Yoshioka's been absent for a while. Our assistant homeroom teacher is running class," said Shun. Shun had the art teacher for homeroom, too. "He said Mr. Yoshioka's sick."

Some third years in the club said that when they peeked into Mr. Yoshioka's office, it had been all tidied up, which almost never happened. "His unfinished paintings even had cloth draped over them," said the club president. That was enough to make everyone worried.

Usually that room was so messy it was as if he lived there. Multiple easels. All sorts of documents piled on his desk. Bookshelves packed with art books, specialized tomes, and magazines. The walls were covered with sketches and notes, too. But there was one wall that had only one panel hanging on it. It was a photo of a big building. The stately Western-style architecture was illuminated by lively lanterns strung all around it for some reason.

Nozomi and her friends went to see Mr. Yoshioka's office for themselves. The door from the hallway was locked. They tried going through the art prep room, but that entrance was locked as well.

"That's weird. He always leaves it open," Shun said, rattling the doorknob. "Maybe it'll be locked until a sub comes."

There was a little window in the door, so they could peek in, but all they could see was that one photo hanging on the wall. In front of that, just as the older kids had said, were two easels with cloth draped over them.

"I wonder if he's all right," said Shun.

It was the next Monday at an all-school assembly that the principal announced, "Mr. Yoshioka is ill and will be taking some time off."

"What illness?"

"I wonder if he got aftereffects."

"Aftereffects, like you mean from the bomb?"

"A-bomb sickness?"

Nozomi could hear the kids in the back row whispering. When she turned around, she saw it was the students from class six, Mr. Yoshioka's class. One of them was Shun and another was Kozo Nonaka, who had gone to the same elementary school as Nozomi.

A quarter century had passed since the end of the war, but there were always people near Nozomi and the others suffering from A-bomb sickness. They weren't all people who had experienced the blast, either. Some were second-generation, children born to people who had experienced it. In elementary school, she had a classmate whose head was terribly small due to radiation, and there were also kids who had died of leukemia. She figured that must have been what Kozo and everyone was talking about.

A-bomb sickness . . . ?

Nozomi suddenly remembered the story she'd heard in the cemetery.

She heard voices again.

"Was he exposed to the bomb?"

"I heard he was exposed when he came into the city—*nyushi hibaku.*"

When he was looking for Satoko, Nozomi thought. *Grandma said they only found her comb or something, right? He kept looking and looking until he found it, so that must be when he was exposed.*

Nozomi had learned the word *"nyushi hibaku"* as an older elementary schooler. She remembered well how the first time she heard it, she didn't know what *"nyushi"* meant—because the written characters didn't pop into her head immediately.

There had been a homework assignment to listen to the story of someone who had experienced the bomb— a *hibakusha*—and that was when she first learned the details.

An uncle explained it—her mother's sister's husband.

This uncle was always joking around and teasing Nozomi, but that time he got serious and said, "You write it with the characters for 'enter' and 'city,'" writing it in a notebook for her. He also taught her the difference between the two words for "exposure," both pronounced *hibaku*.

"When you write *'nyushi hibaku,'* you use the *'hibaku'* with the kanji that means 'exposure' instead of the kanji for 'bomb.'" He explained that the way *"hibaku"* is written depends on whether someone had been affected directly by the bomb or was just exposed to the radiation. There were many people in Hiroshima who had escaped damage at the moment the bomb fell but were exposed to the radiation it left behind after it exploded. Her uncle was one of them.

"No one knew just how frightening this bomb, the flash—*pika*—was. No one ever imagined you would get A-bomb sickness just from walking around the city. But we were actually wandering streets filled with radiation."

The news had said it was a "new type of bomb" or a "special type of bomb," and it wasn't until much later that people learned it was an atomic bomb. All the units that entered the city to clean up were also exposed, and many people died without being properly diagnosed.

The day after the bomb fell, Nozomi's uncle had gone into the center of town to look for his missing elder sister along with a cousin who was looking for his younger sister. The girls were the same age.

When they got to town, it was a scene straight from hell. It was so bad they couldn't believe the sky over their heads was still blue. Charred corpses were scattered all over, and they could hear the groans of people who were still breathing. Here and there, people begged for water, yet water gushed across the scorched earth because pipes had burst. As the two boys walked around under the blazing sun, they drank any number of times.

"Why didn't you give water to the people who were asking for it?" Nozomi asked.

Her uncle answered apologetically. "If you give water to someone with such bad burns, they'll die instantly. We were told to absolutely not give anyone water."

All day long the pair had walked, but their search was all for nothing. The next day, they heard that the girls had been taken to a shelter. When they went to pick them up, neither his sister nor his cousin was still alive.

At the end of August, his cousin developed bruise-like

marks on his body. His hair fell out, he vomited tons of blood, and at the end of his suffering, he died.

Nozomi's uncle had walked the same route and drunk the same water, yet he didn't get sick.

"What happened to us was *nyushi hibaku*. But I still don't know why our fates ended up different like they did," he said. The only thing he could think of was that after that day of walking, he threw up a lot and had diarrhea, too. "Maybe that got the poison out of my body. . . ."

There were an awful lot of people like Nozomi's uncle who weren't harmed by the bomb directly but had became ill from exposure to the lingering radiation. Some people's symptoms came on quickly, while others were struck with the illness long after the bomb had hit.

"It's like an invisible enemy lurking in the night— you never know when it will strike," he said to end the conversation.

"You're all right now, though, right?" Nozomi asked cautiously. "You've been healthy all this time."

Her uncle joked, "I disinfect with alcohol, so I'm all right! I have a drink a day, you know?" But his eyes weren't smiling.

That was the first time Nozomi realized that regardless

of which type of *hibaku* people experienced, they were living their lives in fear of an enemy they couldn't see.

Nozomi's memories of hearing the word *"nyushi hibaku"* as an elementary schooler returned to her. And the image of Mr. Yoshioka in the cemetery from that spring came to mind.

Perhaps her teacher not only had lost someone precious to him, but was battling an invisible enemy as well. She thought of his thin, bony shoulders.

Could Mr. Yoshioka really have A-bomb sickness?

The morning assembly continued, but Nozomi was completely distracted, and she didn't hear a word the teachers were saying.

In the hall as they were on their way back to class, Nozomi caught up with Shun.

"I hope Mr. Yoshioka isn't too sick."

"He seemed healthy. He's just a little skinny. . . . That's different from A-bomb sickness, right?"

Nozomi blurted out what she had been keeping to herself all this time. "So this spring, I actually saw him at the cemetery."

When Shun heard that, he stopped in his tracks, causing the students behind him to complain and go around. Nozomi stopped as well, and the two of them went off to the side by the windows.

"He was visiting the grave plot next to my family's. I guess his fiancée is buried there. She died in the flash, too. And he went looking for her around ground zero. . . ."

As soon as she said it, she regretted it. Maybe it was something personal she shouldn't have shared. But to her relief, Shun simply nodded.

"I know that story. They couldn't find her bones, so they buried her comb."

"Huh? Where did you hear that?"

"My sister told me."

Shun's sister had graduated from the same middle school several years previously and was a member of the art club. She wanted to make a collage of old Japanese combs and hair ornaments, and when she consulted with Mr. Yoshioka, he had suddenly started talking. First about the comb, then about his fiancée, Satoko.

"He gave that comb to her for Jūgoya moon-viewing. It even has a rabbit design inlay."

Nozomi wanted to hear the story right that moment,

but first period was starting. "Tell me the rest after school at art club."

After Shun promised, they each walked to class. Nozomi didn't know how she would concentrate on her studies for the rest of the day.

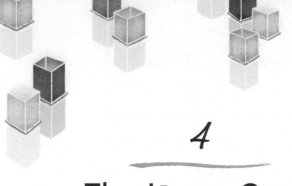

4

The Jūgoya Comb

"*I* found the comb wrapped in washi paper on my mother's vanity. My mother had already passed away. When I gave it to Satoko, she was delighted. She put it in a little pouch and carried it with her everywhere," Mr. Yoshioka had said to Shun's sister, explaining that back then, people didn't have a single pretty thing.

It was such a plain little pouch, sewed from scraps of cotton. But Satoko had said that taking out the boxwood comb and tracing the rabbit image with her finger made her happy. She said that when the war was over, she would put the comb in her hair, and they would go moon-viewing together on Jūgoya.

"We never got to see the harvest moon together

because the next summer the flash got her." And when he'd said, "All we found was the charred comb," the vitality seemed to drain out of him. He stopped talking and walked away.

Shun's sister told Shun and his mother that story. She found a rabbit comb and put it in her collage.

There were lots of small items at the Peace Memorial Museum, too: burned and melted lunch boxes, a *geta* sandal with faint toe marks, a belt buckle, clocks that had stopped at 8:15 a.m.

Some of the owners of the items were known; others not.

The comb with the rabbit inlay was all they'd found to remember Satoko by.

"They didn't find anything else?"

Seventy thousand people had died in an instant beneath the mushroom cloud, and the city was burned to the ground by a raging fire in the blink of an eye. Only things that managed to go unburned in that inferno— things that were sent flying, things that happened to be shielded by other things—only these lucky items that survived a one-in-a-thousand or maybe one-in-ten-thousand chance were found.

Nozomi and the others had studied the bombing in depth since elementary school in their peace studies classes, but it was hard to understand it as something that actually happened. Now that the story was about Mr. Yoshioka, though, events took on a different weight.

Nozomi sighed sadly, and Shun must have felt the same way. He murmured, "Even the things you think you know, you might not know so well after all."

"And the same goes for people."

Nozomi looked at the open space by the window. She noticed that Mr. Yoshioka had cleaned up and his easel was gone.

As far as Nozomi knew, Mr. Yoshioka's easel in the art club room was always in the same place: by the window where he could see the schoolyard—the same window he stood by to see the students off. From that vantage point, he had painted the same scene over and over, never tiring of it. Sometimes he sketched people near the gate. But in the finished paintings, it was always just the empty schoolyard in the foreground and the open gate.

The pictures were practically all the same. Only the

seasons were different: The schoolyard with cherry blossoms in bloom. The schoolyard with the ginkgo trees changing color. But there was never anyone looking up at the cherry blossoms or bending down to pick up a ginkgo leaf. Several of the paintings were stored in the art prep room.

What was he trying to paint? Nozomi wondered. *What was he looking at?*

The art club had a fairly large membership for a non-sports club. Mr. Yoshioka's absence was felt in a big way, but with the help of a substitute supervisor, the third years led club activities during the summer holiday. Everyone was working on major projects for the fall culture festival.

The theme was "Hiroshima: Then and Now."

It had been Shun and Nozomi's idea. They weren't sure if it was all right to share Mr. Yoshioka's personal history with everyone or not, so at first they talked to the other kids about how you might think you know someone, but you actually don't.

And when they did that, they learned that there weren't

many kids who had heard firsthand accounts of the bomb from relatives or people in their neighborhoods—even though most of the students at this middle school were second-generation survivors. Perhaps one reason was that the experiences were so hard that many survivors didn't talk about them.

When Nozomi said, "I didn't know that Mr. Yoshioka was a *nyushi hibaku* victim," lots of the kids nodded. Maybe the reason a proposal from a couple of first years got selected was because everyone was thinking of Mr. Yoshioka.

"It doesn't have to be about the bomb. It could be about Hiroshima during the war, or even before it," said the ponytailed club president, choosing her words carefully.

Then Akiro, the boy who was vice president stood up. "There's that photograph in Mr. Yoshioka's office. Let's go get it."

"Isn't the office locked?" Nozomi asked.

"I bet the door from the prep room is open," Akiro replied.

The office had been locked for a while, but lately the door from the prep room seemed to be open. They had heard that Mr. Yoshioka had asked the school to allow them to use whatever art books and materials they needed.

"A photo of Hiroshima?" Shun and the others were trying to remember what photo the vice president meant. A moment later he brought back the picture that had been hanging on the western wall.

"Do you know what this is a picture of?"

The older kids knew, but Nozomi didn't.

"This is the Atomic Bomb Dome a long time ago— before the bomb dropped."

The younger kids were all stunned.

It was a picture of the Industrial Promotion Hall, what people had nicknamed the *chinretsukan*—the exhibition hall. It was a beautiful building designed by a Czech architect. Nozomi and the others had seen photos of it at the Peace Memorial Museum, of course, but they'd never seen it looking quite as radiant as this. The picture seemed to have been taken during some kind of event or festival. The sun must have been about to go down; lanterns shone beneath a darkening sky. The remaining natural light and the glow of the people's lanterns mixed to wonderful effect.

"I wonder if Mr. Yoshioka took this."

"He says it was a gorgeous modern building."

"I heard that, too. Like, it even had a pipe organ."

Everyone crowded around the photograph. It was impossible to imagine that the tragic frame of the A-Bomb Dome belonged to this grand, elegant building. The lanterns strung around it illuminated it so vibrantly that it seemed like one big shining light. The people in the foreground wore *yukata* or other summer clothes and carried fans.

"There must have been a festival going on."

"Maybe Toukasan?"

"Did they have Toukasan back then?"

"Did they even have festivals during the war?"

The president flipped the panel over, but all that was written on the back was *"Hikari no utsushie."* There was no date.

"'Tracing the light'?"

"'The photograph.'"

"It can indicate a painting, too. When you depict something precious to you."

When the older kids had asked Mr. Yoshioka the

meaning of the word, he had told for the first time the story of what was said to be the origin of the word for "picture." It started from the practice of tracing a traveler's shadow before they left to keep them both in mind and eye. He had opened a catalog and showed them an example of that tradition. It was a picture of a girl touching the outline of her sweetheart on a wall.

"Tracing the light, huh . . . ?"

All the kids looked at the picture. The title seemed even more appropriate now that the gleaming Industrial Promotion Hall was lost forever.

Did Mr. Yoshioka title the picture after the war? Nozomi was thinking, when a third-year boy murmured the same idea. "Maybe he added the title later. To keep the Industrial Promotion Hall in our minds and eyes, and the people there, too, probably."

"Anyone in the neighborhood of the dome probably died instantly."

Everyone looked at the photograph again. Against the backdrop of the modern, majestic building, everyone's faces beamed.

"They look like they're having fun."

"Yeah, it's so cheerful, or like . . ."

"It must be a picture from before the war, huh?"

"And their clothes don't really look like wartime clothes, either."

"Some people even have clean white *yukata*."

"They didn't wear *yukata* during the war?"

"What kind of clothes do you wear during a war?"

Just looking at that photograph brought up all kinds of questions about what Hiroshima used to be like. The kids decided to look things up when they didn't know the answer, and the secretary, a second-year, furiously took notes on their discussion.

"If we painted pictures or created something to show how people lived in Hiroshima before the war . . ."

"Before and during?"

"If I asked my grandma about what things were like back when it was peaceful, I'm sure she can tell me lots of things."

"She'll never stop."

After the excitement died down a little bit, the president summarized their plan.

"So then should we say the idea is to depict Hiroshima before and up through that day?"

"We should concentrate on the people who lived there."

"Including the lives of kids the same age as us."

"Even if kids our age were going to school, they didn't study much—or like, they couldn't. . . ."

Someone joked, "Oh, I'm jealous."

"But art was the first class taken off the schedule when the war started," a third year said.

"They said art and music weren't good for anything."

"I heard that once they started sending students to the front, art school students were the first college students to be rounded up."

Some exclaimed how unfair that was, and everyone got all excited again.

"Art and music students went right away—because people said they were studying something that didn't contribute to the country."

There were a number of kids in the club who wanted to continue on to art school, so this conversation had a big impact.

In the end, the goal became to depict Hiroshima then and now as best they could. All styles and mediums— paintings, sculpture, photographs—were allowed, and they would accept pieces from any of the school's students. They decided this would be the call for submissions: "Hiroshima: Then and Now."

"I'm glad they liked our idea," said Nozomi.

"I thought they might say we were getting ahead of ourselves as first years, but I guess the art club is pretty liberal-minded!" Shun replied happily.

They were leaning against a window. The baseball team was out jogging in the schoolyard. Usually they did twenty laps.

"Look—it's Kozo," Shun remarked. "He sticks out."

Kozo Nonaka was taller than everyone else, so he was easy to pick out of the group of runners. Shun waved at him.

"Kozo loves Mr. Yoshioka and is really worried about him. He keeps telling me we should go visit him and is always asking the health teacher how he's doing."

"That's so like Kozo. . . ."

Nozomi and Kozo had been in the same class for third and fourth grades. They had been on school pet duty together, and while other boys would just go home,

Kozo always stayed after school and helped care for the animals. He would scratch the hens' ears with his big, clumsy-seeming fingers and tear up vegetables for the rabbits. Nozomi remembered thinking that it was mysterious how even the most ill-tempered chickens would tamely allow Kozo to pet them.

"Oh, right, you two went to the same elementary school."

As she was about to ask how Shun knew that, Kozo looked up at them. He pretended to adjust his cap and gave them a little wave.

Shun waved back. Nozomi blushed slightly but waved a bit in front of her chest.

Once they finished their laps, the team scattered around the field.

"Come to think of it, Kozo said his aunt was found as bones," Shun said suddenly. "There were seven people's worth, or something."

"Seven people?"

"His aunt was a teacher, and the flash got her and her students."

So there was something left so they could tell who was who, Nozomi thought.

"Maybe Kozo will paint something for the exhibition. . . ."

"He said he can't paint. I think his elective is music—er, no, maybe calligraphy?"

"Then maybe you could listen to the story and draw something."

"I already have two ideas. I might make one a sculpture. I think I'm going to tell the story of one of my neighbors." Shun paused. "She's kind of a scary lady, but . . ."

"Hmm . . ."

"What about you, Nozomi?"

"I'm . . ." She trailed off. What she really wanted to draw was Mr. Yoshioka and Satoko's story.

When she'd heard the story of the comb, she felt like she could practically see Satoko right in front of her: A young lady taking a comb with a rabbit inlay out of a plain cotton pouch. She must have unfolded the old washi and enjoyed tracing the rabbit's ears with a finger before carefully wrapping it back up and tucking it away. Nozomi could even imagine her looking down with a slightly bashful expression.

She must have been awfully pretty. Artists always have

beautiful muses. I wonder if he ever painted her. Having thought that far, Nozomi remembered that in the identical schoolyard views Mr. Yoshioka painted, there was never so much as a single person present.

Why doesn't he paint people?

"What are you going to paint?" Shun asked again, and Nozomi returned to herself.

"There are a few things I'd like to do. One is the story about the comb. . . . Do you think your sister would give me more details?"

Shun's sister had gone to an art university in Tokyo— one of those schools from which she would have been mobilized right away when the students were called to go to war. It was a tough school to get into.

"She's actually home on summer vacation right now. She might know a little more. I'll ask her for you," said Shun. "And we need to remember to ask Kozo about the bones."

5

The Teacher's Story

During the war, the military had artists paint the battlefield or held festive lantern processions to see soldiers off. The purpose was to boost morale. Many artists reluctantly followed the orders. I was one of them.

I didn't feel comfortable painting military art. But when I was injured and sent home, from the army's point of view, not only was I useless, I was fooling around. I was working as a substitute teacher, but there was a limit to what subjects I was able to teach, so if I got an order from the army, I had no choice but to do what I was told.

I decided I would depict the cruelty of the battlefield.

I figured that if the army questioned me I could get away with it by saying, "I meant to show what a difficult time the soldiers are having."

When I saw a painting by Tsuguharu Foujita at the time, I was encouraged because he seemed to be working with the same feelings as me. *Honorable Death on Attu Island* is a dark, gruesome picture depicting gut-wrenching pain and sadness that seems to spring from the pit of the earth.

But after the war, Foujita was accused of cooperating with the war effort and was practically chased out of the country—he moved to France. How could anyone look at his work and say it was done to boost fighting spirit? I still don't understand.

I lived alone, so Satoko often delivered me a meal at school, and she had done so that day. While I ate, she stared in silence at a half-finished painting. "Why are you painting these things?" she asked me.

I replied coldly, "You can't even understand that much?" I told her, disappointed, that I wasn't doing it because I wanted to—it was my way of protesting with all my might.

Satoko was so genuine and honest; she never

pretended to know something she didn't, instead always asking for an explanation. I loved that about her, and yet I snapped at her.

She looked ashamed.

Finally, she said in a tiny voice that trailed off, "I don't know much about anything, so . . ." and sadly left the art room. I didn't even turn to watch her go.

If she had talked back, said something like, "Look at you on your high horse!" I probably would have apologized immediately, but instead I took advantage of her meekness. I essentially took out my frustration on her.

The hallway was deserted since it was after school, and the sound of her distinctive footsteps echoed in the new *geta* I had recently bought her. I had realized by that point that I was being cruel, but I didn't go after her. I was stuck in my bad mood. As her footsteps receded, though, I suddenly grew anxious and flew out of the classroom. But I didn't see her in the long corridor; she must have already turned to go down the stairs.

I stood rooted to the spot. I couldn't hear any footsteps, so I thought maybe she had sensed I was coming and was waiting for me on the landing. Tensely, I thought, *How should I act? What should I say?*

When I finally turned the corner, no one was there.

Panicked, I raced back to the art room and looked out the window onto the schoolyard. There was Satoko trudging away.

She did look back, just once, but I ducked away from the window. I doubt she saw me.

At the gate, she faced the school, bowed respectfully, and then went home.

I was arrogant and conceited. I thought, *Tomorrow— tomorrow I'll go see her. I'll smile at her as if nothing happened, because I knew she was kind and would forgive me.*

But that was the last time I would see Satoko. And all I could find of her after the bomb fell was the scorched comb.

6

The Lady Looking Up at the Sky in the Field

*E*ver since hearing Mr. Yoshioka's story from Shun's sister, Nozomi had been spending all her time on the picture.

She asked a teacher to let her see the paintings Mr. Yoshioka had left in the office. There were so many with the same composition. They puzzled her, these pictures with no people in them, these pictures he had painted from the same window where he had watched Satoko walk away.

Nozomi put her easel by the window in the space that had been empty ever since Mr. Yoshioka had gone on leave. She thought she would paint the same scene that he had been painting all this time.

After Nozomi listened with such interest to Shun's

sister tell the story and began painting with a focus that astonished the older students, Shun thought, *I blew it. Maybe I should have chosen that story.* Now he was stuck doing the story of a lady in his neighborhood he didn't really get along with, Mrs. Sudo. He wasn't even sure he would be able to get her to talk to him.

As a little kid, he had been afraid of Mrs. Sudo. When his mother told him to take the weekly grocery store flyer over, he would go reluctantly. Mrs. Sudo was always at home.

Shun had never heard her voice. Even if he said hello, she only nodded a bit, moving her slightly jutting chin. She was like that with everyone in the neighborhood. They all thought she was a bit strange.

Mrs. Sudo was a tailor and spent all day at either her work table or her sewing machine. Her workshop was in the half of her two-room house facing the street, and her sewing machine sat in the window. When approaching her house, Shun could sense her looking at him even as her sewing fingers never stopped moving. And she always took the flyer through the window, extending her arm sporting a pincushion that looked like a bracelet with marking pins sticking out.

The road in front of Mrs. Sudo's house was the way to the local elementary and middle schools. When Shun walked to school, she was always watching out the window. She watched all the kids in their little groups go by. And on their way home, too.

When it was nice out, she left the window open, and he could see into her workshop. Sometimes he would catch a glimpse of a half-finished garment on a mannequin. A floral-print dress, a suit the color of the sky in spring. The flashy outfits drew attention, of course, and Shun had heard grown-ups talking about them more than once.

"She makes such pretty clothes, but why never for herself?" His father's younger sister, his aunt Atsuko, had said that to his grandmother. Mrs. Sudo always wore a faded smock with a kerchief wrapped around her neck. And then the wristband pincushion. Shun didn't think she looked like someone who made pretty clothes.

"She probably has plenty of leftover fabric, too," his aunt had continued, but his grandmother remained silent for a moment before responding in a quiet voice, "I feel so bad for her."

Shun had been curious why, but he had plans to play

baseball with his friends, so he rushed out of the house. He learned the reason as a middle schooler. He heard his grandmother talking to his aunt Atsuko again.

Atsuko had gone over to share some food with Mrs. Sudo and came back bad-mouthing her. "She couldn't even say hello properly. What a strange woman!"

His grandmother snapped back, "If you're going to complain like that, then why take anything over at all? If you were all alone in the world with no one to talk to, you might understand how she feels."

The older woman was usually so calm that her harshness shut Atsuko up.

"You even know a little about her circumstances, so honestly . . ." With that, she stood up and left the room.

When Atsuko realized Shun was there, she stuck her tongue out at him.

His aunt Atsuko was his father's youngest sister. She was only a little older than her nephew. To Shun, she was more like an older sister than an aunt. She was easygoing, often whining that she wanted to hurry up and get married so she could get out of the house. She was in her mid-twenties and hadn't managed to meet anyone yet.

"I made her mad again."

"What did she mean when she said that Mrs. Sudo has no one to talk to . . . ?"

"The *pika* got him. The flash got her adorable little first-grader son. I don't know the details, though."

Shun recalled how she watched the elementary and middle schoolers go past her window.

"Sadly, her husband was also killed in the war down south," Atsuko added when Shun said nothing. "Your grandma is right—I was thoughtless. It must be awfully hard to live all alone in this world. . . ."

Shun lived in a cheerful household with not only his parents, but his grandmother and aunt, too. Being utterly alone sounded awful.

"Ah, I need to hurry up and get married, make a family of my own." Atsuko repeated her usual line and left him.

When Nozomi had said to him that sometimes you might not know people as well as you think you do, he had wondered if that was really true. It was definitely the case when it came to Mrs. Sudo.

It was the same for Mr. Yoshioka. Shun would never

have guessed that something so tragic had happened to their teacher when he was younger. You couldn't imagine it from his smile, the way he sometimes joked around, or the way he took up his brush and taught them with such care.

Mrs. Sudo took the flyer with such a frightening look on her face. She was all alone. Shun wondered what had happened to her little boy that day. What had happened to her? He figured his grandmother knew the details.

That weekend when Shun and his grandmother were at home, he asked about Mrs. Sudo.

His grandmother was slightly taken aback.

"Why do you want to know about that?"

"The art club is doing projects about Hiroshima, so I thought if it was okay for me to hear the story, I'd like to. Like for example . . ." Shun told her about Mr. Yoshioka and the story he had heard from his sister.

She nodded, sewing as she listened, but then stopped and took her glasses off. She was looking down, pretending to wipe them, but she was crying.

"That pain and sadness . . . Mrs. Sudo has the same sort of painful regrets that Mr. Yoshioka does." She looked her grandson straight in the eye. She was moved because she had thought he was still a child, yet he took this story of his teacher's past to heart in a deep way.

That afternoon his grandmother agreed to tell him the story of what had happened to Mrs. Sudo's only son, Kenji.

A year after that August 6 morning, Mrs. Sudo collapsed on the riverside and was taken on a stretcher to a clinic. It was a scorching hot summer day. Mrs. Sudo fell unconscious, and since she had no family, Shun's grandmother ended up taking care of her.

"The doctor at the clinic asked me to since I lived next door and had a reputation for being helpful."

Shun's family house had land around it that was quite spacious, so even before the war they had often taken people in. When the bomb dropped, too, they set up thirty students from the local middle school in their shed and looked after them. Most of them didn't make it. That was a different story, though, so his grandmother continued Mrs. Sudo's.

"At that time Mrs. Sudo was terribly thin, so much so that I worried she might breathe her last right there. It seemed like she hadn't been eating. The doctor at the clinic scolded her. 'You survived, so you can't waste your life like this.' "

Shun's grandmother cocked her head and thought for a moment.

"Of course, all I could say was, 'You never know when Kenji might come home, so you have to hang in there and wait for him.' What a lame consolation."

No matter what the doctor, his grandmother, or anyone else said to her, she simply lay there without a word of reply and went home a week later.

"At the end of the summer, perhaps she'd had a change of heart, because she started up her sewing business. A year later, we found a summer dress she'd sewn and left at the back door. It was good, careful work. There was a note tucked into the breast that said 'Thank you.' "

When Shun's grandmother went to thank her, Mrs. Sudo seemed very uncomfortable and just insisted that she go home.

"She has a hard time communicating with people; she's too wounded emotionally. And since she doesn't have anyone to talk to, I think she forgets how to use her voice."

"Can that really happen . . . ?"

"Try not talking to anyone for a week."

Shun tried to imagine it. He wasn't much of a chatter-box, but by the end of a week, he felt like he would probably talk like a dam had broken.

"I'd probably talk forever after that. . . ."

"About nothing in particular? Maybe."

Shun nodded. Sometimes, when he got really sad, he couldn't get words out. It had been like that when their dog had died. He couldn't even cry. But when he saw the empty kennel, or saw other healthy dogs walking around, his chest tightened. If Mrs. Sudo had been living with that feeling for years and years, then Shun could understand. And of course, there's a difference between losing a dog and losing a young son.

"I thought it would be best to leave her be, so although I kept her in my thoughts, I didn't prod her much, but . . ."

Then several years later, she saw Mrs. Sudo. It was the middle of the night, and she happened to look out the window from the second floor.

Mrs. Sudo was standing in a field looking up at the sky.

It was a cold, cold winter night, the kind when it

seems like the stars are frozen in the sky. Moonlight shone down, casting Mrs. Sudo's shadow on the dried-up grass.

"I thought, *She's really all alone in the world.* I realized that night that I couldn't just leave her alone. So I rolled some sushi and went to see her the next day."

Shun's grandmother made great sushi rolls. Eel roasted crispy, sweet simmered *kanpyō,* plus *mitsuba* and egg, all rolled up—everyone loved her sushi.

"I said, 'No one's home all of a sudden, and it's lonely to eat by myself. Would you eat with me?'"

Perhaps it was the way she invited her? Mrs. Sudo came over without a fuss. She seemed to be really enjoying the sushi when suddenly, she began to cry.

His grandmother had stood up and made some roasted green tea. Then the two of them warmed themselves by the charcoal heater and sipped the hot drink.

That was when Mrs. Sudo slowly began to speak—it was probably the first time she had opened her heart—about what had happened that day, the days after that, and her lonely life afterward.

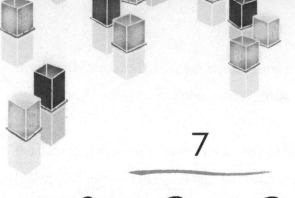

7

Mrs. Sudo's Story

I was wondering where Kenji was, since it was time for him to leave, and I found him playing in the yard again. He couldn't help himself—he just loved the lily-pad pot and the killifish in the old urn.

"You're going to be late for school!" When I called him, he turned around, still crouched down, but I must have startled him, because he spilled the contents of the wooden bowl in his hand all over himself. He'd been stirring up the lily-pad pot.

I had just dressed him in the freshly washed uniform, but now there was green algae water all over both his shirt and his pants.

Kenji slumped his way over to me.

"I just put you in those clean clothes."

He only hung his head in silence.

"Honestly, I can't believe you!"

Kenji tugged at the hem of his shirt with a pathetic look on his face. His pants were covered in mud.

After wiping him off, I smacked him on the bottom and hustled him off. I was going to be late for my labor service for the war effort, too, so I was in a rush.

"Just go as you are or you won't make it in time."

Kenji picked his bag up off the entryway step, slung it across his body, and left without saying anything. I think he turned around once at the corner, but I didn't look. I was still angry. I don't even think I said *Be careful* or *See you later*. Or maybe I did at least say *See you later*. . . . I don't remember.

It really wasn't such a big deal that he got his clothes dirty.

Why couldn't I have just said *Sheesh, Kenji—oh, well. C'mon, now. Get going*?

Was it because I was sleep-deprived from the incessant warnings that continued until dawn? Was it the stress of never knowing what the next day would bring? Was it the lack of news from my husband away on the battlefield? But those were all just excuses. None of them were any reason to be cold to a child.

The flash hit only a little while later that morning. By the time I could run to the first-aid station, Kenji was already gone. His body was burned and melted, his face terribly swollen. I couldn't believe it was him. But the bit of his shirt that wasn't burned up had an algae stain.

After about a year, I started having the same dream over and over. I dreamed that my son came home.

Was that dead body really Kenji? Maybe what I thought was an algae stain was just some other kind of dirt.

Nothing else—neither his holey shoes nor the bag he had carried—was found. The teacher who told me, "This is Kenji," also died.

Was it really him?

The horrible doubt and pained hope wouldn't leave my mind.

Maybe Kenji was alive; maybe he had survived and was living somewhere. Could he be in the shacks by the riverside, huddled with the other A-bomb orphans?

Did he forget in the flash that he had a mother and a house to go home to?

When I had that thought, I couldn't take it anymore, and the next thing I knew, I found myself in the riverside slum.

It was so, so hot out that day that I collapsed, and Mrs. Nakamura took care of me. I couldn't even thank her properly. I feel bad about that. I had such little willpower that I couldn't get my head or my tongue to work right. I had lost the energy to live long ago.

But it was just as the doctor at the clinic said: "If you've survived, you've got to live. No matter how hard it is, you have to keep on living until your time comes."

I repeated his words over and over to myself and decided to make a living sewing. Still, I was so lonely I couldn't stand it. Eventually, the tears stopped coming and I just passed my days in a daze. I couldn't even cry, I felt so empty.

That was when a poem in the newspaper caught my eye. I think it was around Children's Day.

My little boy came back with dirtied shorts. I scolded him, and the next thing I knew he had died in the war.

It was a tanka by Hitomi Koyama.

When I read that poem, I finally cried. I remember being surprised as my tears fell and wet blotches spread across the paper.

My only son never came home. Then one day, I received an empty wooden box and a slip of paper telling me this sad news: my husband had died fighting in the south, who knows where. I was left completely alone in the world.

Ever since that day, I had lived without a soul to talk to. I'd been able to get by with my sewing, but I lived without hope.

Now here was someone else living with thoughts of a son who would never return. From then on, I waited each week for the day the tanka were printed.

Hitomi Koyama's poems were selected almost every week. What I learned from them was that she was alone like me, that she made enough to live as a peddler, and that she carried her dead son in her heart always.

I copied her poems into a notebook. Sometimes I was so lonely it was hard to breathe, but I'm sure opening that notebook gave me some consolation.

As I sleep alone on nights when snow is quietly falling, I feel as though my boy's soul is tapping at my window

Perhaps this endless blue of the sky is the color that connects me to my fallen boy

There are probably more mothers like Mrs. Koyama and me in this world than we can count, no distinguishing between enemies and allies; I'm sure that in America, in China, Korea, and Europe, there are mothers living their days the same way as me, breath by breath.

I'm just an uneducated woman, and I don't know much, but even I know that somewhere in this world there is still fighting going on, and mothers are losing their precious children. . . .

The reason I was looking up at the sky that night was because I was thinking that that same sky stretches over all those mothers.

I've never met Mrs. Koyama, and I don't even know the names of the others. How many are there like us, who had no idea their children would part so soon, who scolded them, or were cold to them, who couldn't feed them as well as they wanted to, who carry those regrets in their hearts? That's what I was thinking as I looked up at the sky.

And I wondered what I would say if I could go back to that morning.

Would I chase after him and shower him with tickles, saying, *You naughty boy. This is the last time I'll be able to forgive you!* as we laughed? Or would I smack his bottom and tell him, *All right, get going and I'll see you later?* Or would I say, *Sorry I got mad at you. . . . Be careful on your way and get home safely?*

The thing that really hit home in Mrs. Koyama's poems was the regret I could hear in the one about the shorts: being alive here with me would have been enough.

8

Sanitarium

By the time Shun's grandmother finished Mrs. Sudo's story, the sun had gone down. He thanked her and went to his room, but then decided to go back and ask her about the poem.

She wrote it neatly on the piece of paper he gave her.

My little boy came back with dirtied shorts. I scolded him, and the next thing I knew he had died in the war.

"Such a sad poem. Luckily I didn't lose any children . . . but there must be countless mothers in the world who feel this way." She patted Shun's shoulder. "I can be harsh with you sometimes, only because I

71

trust you'll come back in one piece tomorrow and the next day."

Shun hung the poem facing his desk and took out his sketchbook. He'd been drawing large pictures in it ever since the spring, but he wanted to try his hand at sculpture. To start, he thought he would sketch the story he'd just heard.

First he tried drawing a boy. It didn't come out very well, so he took a magazine off his bookshelf. He couldn't find any pictures of small boys.

What shape is a lily-pad pot, again?

Someone would have one out in front of their house; or if nothing else, he could look it up at the library. As he was thinking that maybe they would have photo books with pictures of young children, too, he remembered Nozomi's little brother. If memory served, he was still in the early years of elementary school.

Is he a second grader? Or is it third? Maybe if I ask, she'll let me sketch him.

Having made up his mind to ask Nozomi, he began to sketch: A figure in a soiled shirt peering into the lily-pad pot, clearly on the verge of tears. And with that same face, the figure turning around at the corner.

For a while, Shun focused his entire being on drawing. But suddenly he felt like he was being watched. When he looked up, there was a big full moon out the window on his left. He could see the field in the moonlight. It was the field his grandmother had mentioned, the one Mrs. Sudo had stood in, looking up at the sky.

Shun and his friends had played there often when they were younger. Houses had gone up around it, but the field remained. The owner of the land must have had some reason for holding on to it, but Shun had heard older women in the neighborhood saying, "The owner doesn't have much time left, so I imagine it'll be sold before long." It had been years since then and the owner was still healthy, so the field remained, overgrown. The summer weeds had been left to grow wild and were swaying under the moonlight.

There was a row house across the field. Mrs. Sudo's place was the second door from the left. It wasn't even nine o'clock yet, but the lights were out. *Is she already asleep? Or is she out somewhere looking up at the sky?* When Shun started thinking like that, he grew depressed.

He took the half-finished sketch and left his room.

Downstairs he could hear the television and his aunt laughing. His grandmother was saying something.

When he descended a couple of steps, he could smell the bath. His father must have been taking one. And it must have been his mother making the clinking noises in the kitchen.

It was a normal night at his house—the usual smells, the usual sounds—yet something felt different. Gradually, Shun realized that the difference was his own feelings. He was upset by the thought that the people his grandmother had mentioned, those who live their lives with no one to talk to, might already have turned off their lights and started their long, dark night. And he thought about more people alone and lonely.

Shun opened the sliding door and peeked into the living room at his family.

His father had just come out of the bath and joined them. He seemed to be in a good mood. But there were hard keloids and burn marks on his hand, and in his heart, he probably carried the friends he'd lost. Shun was shocked to find himself realizing that only now and felt moved by all that must have happened to so many people he loved. He vowed to finish his sculpture of Kenji.

Nozomi, and then Shun, immersed themselves in their projects all summer until vacation ended; now it was September. They had heard news of Mr. Yoshioka over the break—he would not be returning; the sub would be coming again that semester.

The day after the ceremony to welcome everyone back, Nozomi ran into Shun and Kozo talking in the hall.

"Good timing," said Kozo with a smile.

"We're thinking of going to visit Mr. Yoshioka, so we wanted to talk to you."

"Do you want to come, Nozomi?"

Nozomi nodded eagerly. She would be happy to see their teacher, and she was happy that Kozo had invited her.

When Kozo had gone to inquire at the faculty office during the first semester, he learned that Mr. Yoshioka had tuberculosis and was staying in a sanitarium in the suburbs; no visitors would be allowed for some time. The school nurse had said she would let him know when they were clear to visit, so Kozo went to the nurse's office now and then for an update. He'd finally been given permission to visit.

The three of them agreed to meet Sunday morning at the bus stop nearest the school.

Kozo supposedly asked some other people, but the only two who showed up at the bus stop were him and Nozomi.

"Maybe I set the meeting time too early," said Kozo, looking uncharacteristically glum.

"Because school just started, you mean? They're all sleeping in because they're still on summer vacation time? But they said they wanted to see Mr. Yoshioka."

The third years from art club had wanted to come, too, but they had exams.

"Maybe we should have switched days," said Kozo. He looked upset. He had wanted to visit as soon as possible, which was why he had decided so quickly on this day.

"But if too many people showed up, we'd be in the way, anyhow. My mom was saying it would be nicer to have small groups go every now and then rather than have everyone rushing him at once."

Nozomi's response cheered Kozo up. "Okay."

"But I wonder what happened to Shun." *Maybe I should have called him,* thought Nozomi.

They let two buses go by while they waitcd.

"We can wait all we want, but probably no one else is coming." Kozo turned to look at Nozomi. "Wanna just go?"

Nozomi nodded. She was nervous to go as just the two of them, but she wasn't against the idea.

The next bus arrived, and they agreed to get on. Just as they were boarding, someone shouted, "Waaaait!"

It was Shun. He climbed aboard, all out of breath, and grinned. "I overslept!"

So all three of them headed to the sanitarium outside town.

The bus schedule had them arriving after lunch, so Nozomi's mother had given her rice balls to take. They munched on them sitting in a row on the bus, watching as the scenery out the windows started to include more and more green. Kozo happily accepted the last one.

Mr. Yoshioka had just finished his lunch when they arrived, and he was surprised to see them.

"You guys came all the way out here? It took three hours, didn't it?"

"The mountains were pretty," said Nozomi.

"And the fields."

When Nozomi presented Mr. Yoshioka with a box of fruit from their mothers, he looked even more grateful.

The sanitarium was run by a Catholic church, and nuns in crisp white veils bustled around taking care of all the patients.

Mr. Yoshioka looked healthier than Nozomi had expected. He signaled the nuns and then took the three of them out into the garden, which was large and well-tended.

"So was it the bomb that made you sick, Mr. Yoshioka?"

"Hmm . . . if that were the case, I think I might have gotten leukemia, not tuberculosis." Leukemia, or cancer of the blood, was common among people who had been exposed to radiation. "I'm one of the lucky ones," he remarked, and then tousled Kozo's hair as if to say that was enough about being sick. "How's baseball going? Are you doing your best out there?"

Kozo reported on the activities of their underdog baseball team, making it funny.

Mr. Yoshioka laughed aloud. Their teacher was tan even though he was sick. *Maybe that's what makes him look healthier than we expected,* Nozomi thought.

Shun listened in silence, but when Mr. Yoshioka asked what he was painting for the culture festival, he answered that he was challenging himself with a canvas that was almost bigger than he was.

"Even just putting on the undercoat was a lot of work."

"What did you paint?"

"It's supposed to depict Hiroshima from before and now, with the dome, but I'm not sure if I pulled it off or not."

Shun told Mr. Yoshioka how their theme for the festival was "Hiroshima: Then and Now." "And the subtitle is 'Ask people close to you what happened that day.'"

"Hiroshima, huh?"

"I'm also doing a sculpture."

"What's the subject of the sculpture?"

"The son of a lady in my neighborhood. He left that morning and never came back. The lady's been living all alone ever since."

Mr. Yoshioka blinked at Shun's answer and then said,

"I see. . . . Take your time. Be confident and work deeply as you sculpt."

Shun nodded.

"And what about you, Nozomi?"

"I . . ." She exchanged glances with Shun. After hesitating, she finally said, "I'm painting you, Mr. Yoshioka, you and Satoko. . . ."

Nozomi trailed off, so Shun helped her out. "She heard the story from my sister."

"I see."

Nozomi wanted to cry—because she realized, though it was too late now, that she should have asked Mr. Yoshioka's permission before starting to paint.

"Umm . . . if I shouldn't have done that, I don't have to submit it to the festival."

"No, Satoko might be happy to have you paint her." Realizing Nozomi was on the brink of tears, he followed up with a question. "So what are you using? What materials, I mean?"

Nozomi was half crying by now, but she felt slightly relieved and answered, "Oils. It's really difficult."

"Nozomi's working really hard on it. The older kids

are surprised how well it's turning out. You'll be surprised, too, Mr. Yoshioka," added Shun, and Nozomi was finally able to smile.

Then Kozo started telling a story about how he and the other kids from the baseball team had gotten chased by the janitor with a broom for misbehaving. They had not gotten along.

"That old guy's so scary."

"He's fast for such a geezer. If he caught us, we would have been punished."

Just then, a young nun came over. "You seem to be enjoying yourself, Mr. Yoshioka. But the wind has picked up, so how about we return to your room? We have a snack for your students, too."

Mr. Yoshioka said there was a French nun in charge of the kitchen and that the food was delicious. The snacks were usually rare Western cakes.

And what they received really was something Nozomi had never seen before.

"It's called a *pomme de terre,* an 'apple of the earth,'" the same young nun explained. "It doesn't look very appetizing, but it's really tasty."

Oh, it looks just like a potato. It was coated in ground cinnamon, and the parts that looked like eyes were cloves.

"Clothes?" Kozo blinked.

"Not 'clothes,' 'cloves.' It's a type of spice."

Kozo didn't seem to like it very much, but he still gobbled it up. Nozomi and Shun took their time, savoring it. It was the first time they'd ever tasted anything like it.

To drink they had fresh milk from a nearby ranch. Kozo gulped his down and asked for seconds from what was left in the pitcher.

As they were about to leave, Mr. Yoshioka soaked his hands in the little sink in his room, carefully disinfecting each finger. Then he turned around and grinned.

"They said I'm fine, but just in case." Then he offered his hand to the three kids. "Let's shake." After giving them each a firm, two-handed handshake, he sent them off cheerfully. "And don't come again!"

As the bus left the parking lot, they had a good view of Mr. Yoshioka's window. He was watching them go.

"Look, his teeth are shining."

Their teacher was grinning with his teeth showing as he waved.

"He's got such dark skin."

"Everyone at the sanitarium was so fair."

"He's always been that healthy tan color."

Whenever Nozomi thought of their teacher, she thought of his white teeth practically popping out of his dark face when he smiled. Shun and Kozo must have, too. Probably everyone from the art club and their grade felt that way. The reason they were all so surprised to hear he was sick was that they always thought of him with that bright, peppy smile.

But when Nozomi saw him at Mitaki, he had been like a different person. Ever since then, she found herself remembering the sight of him from behind as he limped down that path.

She pictured his expression as he'd said, "And don't come again!" and waved at them today and tried to replace the memory of seeing him from behind at the cemetery. And when the sight of him washing his hands so carefully at the sanitarium came to mind, she found her eyes filling with tears.

Even if he had to disinfect his hands, he wanted to say a proper farewell to everyone. He watched us until we disappeared from view. Because there might not be a tomorrow. Because we might never see each other again. Because he still regrets not going after Satoko.

Her tears startled the two boys.

"Why're you crying?" asked Shun.

"He'll be back as soon as he's better . . . ," said Kozo.

Nozomi wanted to say, *No, that's not it. That's not why,* but she couldn't manage it; her tears just kept falling.

9

The Story Kozo Heard

Kozo was surprised when Nozomi started crying on the way home from the sanitarium. But when he heard Mr. Yoshioka's story from Shun, he felt like crying, too.

He remembered the buzz that had gone through the room when he had started middle school and Mr. Yoshioka had walked into the classroom. Kozo was stunned, too. Mr. Yoshioka was unlike any teacher he'd had in elementary school.

The first surprise was his casual appearance. And the way his writing looked on the blackboard, more like pictures he had drawn than characters (putting it generously), was also a shock. All the teachers he'd had up to that point wrote exactly like the examples in their penmanship textbooks.

When they voted on their class representatives, Mr. Yoshioka had mostly stared out the window, occasionally yawning. Every time one of the more serious girls asked him something, he replied, "You guys can decide."

Kozo thought maybe he was a bit of a slacker for a teacher until one day the boys who had gone to Nishimachi Elementary and the boys who had gone to Higashimachi got in a fight. Mr. Yoshioka said, "If you have to fight, can you at least do it one-on-one? I'll be the referee," and instead of breaking up the fight, he pulled a chair over and sat in front of them. His expression was the same placid one he had when he gazed out the window. Kozo thought it looked like he might yawn at any moment.

Once the bite had gone out of the boys, he really did yawn and then went away.

Shun Nakamura seemed to have been observing their teacher, same as Kozo. "He's always alert when he's painting," the boy said. Kozo asked and found out that Shun was in the art club, so he saw Mr. Yoshioka after school, too.

"And he's always so lax."

"Yeah, he lets anything go."

"I don't really get it, but . . ."

By the end of the first month, Kozo had learned that Mr. Yoshioka didn't like putting restraints on students or giving orders. He probably also hated the idea of just setting an example to be copied.

"He's different from the others because he's an art teacher. He doesn't seem worried about grades or class ranks," one boy had said, as if he knew everything. "Will he be able to write a proper letter of recommendation when we need one?"

That didn't feel right to Kozo. And he'd heard a story from Shun about a third-year girl who used to have Mr. Yoshioka. When the girl had been fighting with her parents about the high school she wanted to go to, Mr. Yoshioka rode his bicycle over to their house and bowed repeatedly, saying, "Please, please understand." That shut the parents up.

"All he did was beg. He didn't use any logic or anything. Total persuasive power: zero."

"But the parents gave in."

Kozo thought it was a very Mr. Yoshioka story—although he wasn't sure himself what made it "very."

When Mr. Yoshioka was coming toward him, Kozo felt like it was a faint wind walking over. A breeze with a limp.

Kozo didn't have the vocabulary to come up with the word "aloof" to describe him, but when he heard the other teachers talk about Mr. Yoshioka that way, he thought it made sense. Still, for some reason—he wasn't sure why—Kozo really liked Mr. Yoshioka.

Hearing that when Mr. Yoshioka was younger, he had lost his beloved, and that he still visited her grave to this day, girls might find it romantic, but Kozo was reminded of something his grandfather said when speaking of the old days: "So many people's fates were changed by the flash. Many of those who survived physically were dead inside."

Maybe his grandfather was one of them. Everyone said he'd aged all at once after losing his daughter to the bomb.

Once his grandmother got on the topic, she would never stop talking: "Sumi." She was his father's sister, seven years older, so to Kozo, she was an aunt. The first summer after she became a teacher, she was a victim of the flash.

Shun had told him over summer vacation about the art club's theme for the culture festival and urged him to listen to the story of someone close to him, but he had gotten busy with baseball and forgotten all about it. Hearing Mr. Yoshioka's story, though, made him think. And he remembered his aunt Sumi.

From what he had heard, she was exactly as purehearted as the kanji for her name—"clear and serene"—implied. His grandmother always bragged that everyone praised her as not only academically skilled but a good girl through and through.

His grandfather didn't boast as openly as his grandmother, but neither did he stop her once she got going; he sat and listened in silence. Eventually, he would start to look sad, and at some point, he would leave the room. That was how it always happened.

A photo of his aunt Sumiko was displayed in the family altar room. It was up above the door with pictures of other ancestors he didn't know. Kozo had seen the picture ever since he was a little boy. The plump cheeks and bright eyes made her look like a student. She seemed only slightly older than Nozomi. He heard the photo had been taken the year she became a teacher. It made more sense to him to call her "Sumi" than "Aunt Sumiko."

Kozo's dad told him, "Sumi would pick up anything out lying around."

"Lying around? You mean like trash?"

"Living things."

Sumi would bring home dogs, cats, baby birds, or even bats—anything that had fallen down or been abandoned. She couldn't just walk by. That was one thing before the war, when life was more comfortable, but during the war when there wasn't enough of anything to go around, she felt judged and secretly kept the animals in the shed.

"I peeked into the shed and the place was crawling with kittens. I couldn't believe my eyes!"

"Yes, yes, and she would give them her own food," his grandmother, who had been listening in silence, chimed in with a tearful smile. "She was such a kind girl."

But when the war got worse, dogs and cats were taken away and killed.

"She sobbed, 'This is madness. It's not fair!'" his

grandmother said, petting the black cat in her lap. The cat was old, and the luster had gone from her coat; she cracked her eyes open and licked the elderly woman's fingers before dozing off again. "Because pets are family, too."

From those stories, Kozo had a good idea of what Sumi was like, but he still didn't have a clear understanding of what had happened to her the day the bomb fell.

It's just like Shun and Nozomi said. Even when you think you know someone, there are tons of things you have no idea about. It was the same with Mr. Yoshioka. I should try asking about Aunt Sumiko and get the whole story.

It was the night they returned from visiting the sanitarium that he thought that.

He waited for a time both his grandparents were in the living room drinking tea to peek in.

When he asked to hear the details about Sumiko, they weren't upset at all, but began to talk happily. First his grandmother repeated the stories he had heard before.

Sumi had been vice president of her class all through elementary school. Back then, class representatives were decided by grades, not voted on. She was always first in her class, so she should have been president, but at that time, the rule was that only a boy could be president. It was such a shame. Kozo's grandfather said that he'd always thought, *Things would have been different if she were a boy.*

After graduating first in her class, she had moved on to R Girls' High. She got only one imperfect grade; otherwise she got what you would call "straight As" nowadays. It was actually her habit of doing her homework right away that got her in trouble: she had written her New Year's calligraphy assignment before the old year had ended. When the teacher asked her when she did it and she answered honestly, her grade was lowered.

Whenever Kozo's grandmother told this story, she would always jokingly lament, "How honest do you have to be?" Then his grandfather would grumble, "If you had only told her to wait till the New Year . . ." To which she would retort, "She just took care of everything so quickly, I didn't even notice," and then keep talking. This night was no different from usual.

Sumi had graduated from R Girls' High with excellent grades and advanced to a teachers' college for women in Nara. And when she graduated from there, she went straight back to her old school to teach. The students all loved her because she was young and kind, like an older sister.

It was around that point in the story that Kozo's grandfather would normally disappear. Then his grandmother would finish up by boasting about how good Sumi had been at needlework, so this night was the first time Kozo had heard about how she died.

His grandfather seemed reluctant to speak, but nonetheless told him what had happened that day and afterward.

10

Big Bones and
Little Bones

The girls' school Sumi was teaching at was a ways from ground zero, but on the morning the bomb dropped, the students were in the center of town. They were out demolishing buildings as part of the student mobilization.

That afternoon, breaking free from everyone who tried to stop him, Kozo's grandfather went out to ground zero as it burned. But the flames were too strong, so he couldn't proceed any farther after a certain point. It was only the next day that he was able to go search around the demolition site.

As he was looking around, something caught his eye. It was a skull surrounded by smaller skulls.

Bones were all that remained. A board set up next to them had a message written in ash: *R Girls' School teacher and students. Burned to death.* Whoever it was hadn't been able to save them, but they must have wanted to at least leave some information. There were other boards nearby; one said *2 Z Middle School students taken to Hijiyama for first aid.*

With the seven skulls on his mind, he nonetheless went to the first-aid station with a glimmer of hope. But he was told that everyone from R Girls' School was gone. Some students and faculty had been brought in for treatment, but almost all of them died on day one. All their names in the register had "deceased" written after them. He looked through the register multiple times but didn't see an entry for Sumiko Nonaka.

The sun was going down, but he circled back to the seven skulls. He was just hoping—praying—that no one had cleaned them up yet.

A memory of a spring afternoon stuck in his mind.

A group of quiet, serious girls with braids stood nervously at the gate of the Nonakas' house. They were elementary schoolers from the district Sumi taught in.

There were six in all.

"There was nothing fun happening for Hina Matsuri, so I thought I'd at least bring them by to see the peach blossoms."

The house had three peach trees and they were in full bloom.

They had dolls and the other festival props stored safely in the cellar, but they hadn't put them up once since the war had begun.

And then, how cheerful it was on the porch! Sumi stood surrounded by the girls, and they were all giggling nonstop.

"They were laughing so much I wondered what could possibly be so funny."

"And they were overjoyed to eat the *oshiruko* I threw together at the last minute."

That morning before Sumi left she had said, "Mother, please boil the red beans. Don't forget." She had started soaking what little azuki they had left the night before. "What little" because it was only about a handful of beans.

"I didn't have time to ask her what it was for, but I couldn't let them go to waste. They were already soaking, so I boiled them."

The plan was to make the sweet red bean soup for the girls.

"Even just a tiny bit of sugar is fine . . . ," Sumi had begged, pressing her palms together, and of course her mother nodded. The girls were so cute, and she was so touched, that she brought out her precious stash of sugar.

It was the thinnest, weakest *oshiruko* you could imagine, but the girls were thrilled. One even started to cry.

Kozo's grandmother was lost for words for a moment. "It was hardly anything . . . but they were so happy."

Though there was no proof, Kozo's grandfather was convinced the seven people's bones that remained after the fire were his daughter, Sumiko, and the girls who had come to see the peach blossoms. She had probably been trying to lead them home.

"I figured that they must have been caught up in a huge blaze, and when they were unable to move any farther, they were burned to death huddled together like that."

He did his best to commit their surroundings to

memory and then carefully wrapped up the bones. He took them all home with him.

They buried the bones that seemed to be Sumiko and put the little skulls in plain wooden boxes for safe-keeping. The school was burned to the ground, so all the records had been lost, but due to the incredible efforts of the few remaining faculty members, the student register was re-created in no time. Having learned the names and addresses of six girls who shared the same walk to school, Kozo's grandfather went around to visit each household.

All of them had lost a beloved daughter and had found no trace of her despite their searching.

When he told them about where he had found the bones and the circumstances—"I think they must be Sumiko and the girls"—the families listened.

Some parents spoke of how their girls talked about how fun and secure they felt walking to school with their teacher, and one mother said over and over how happy her daughter had been on the day of Hina Matsuri. So four families accepted bones.

Of the two remaining bones, one family couldn't be found. It seemed that the flash had gotten them all. Or perhaps they had left town. The house he visited had already been cleaned up, and although there were messages about where to contact other people, he didn't find one for them.

The family of the final student refused to accept the bones. Her mother seemed to be the only one left.

"You don't know if she's really gone. . . . She could come back today," the woman had said curtly. "If I accept these bones, it's like I'm saying I'll never see her again. . . . Please understand."

When this mother told him her feelings, *Please understand,* he could see that her heart was about to snap in two. "Right. She could come back anytime . . . ," he answered, and quickly withdrew.

"I wasn't sure if I had done a good thing or a bad thing. When I started wondering if that was really Sumiko and the girls, there were nights I couldn't sleep."

Kozo's grandfather pretended to blow his nose.

"Then a witness appeared. Someone reported to the school that they had seen 'Miss Nonaka' fleeing with six students and that shortly after that, they had been engulfed in flames."

The surface temperature at ground zero rose to over seven thousand degrees, and all the buildings within about a one-and-a-quarter-mile radius were blown over and immediately began to burn. The fire spread in the blink of an eye, and people in the area were devoured by the violent blaze.

Kozo's grandfather went to visit the witness to hear the details. How they were all badly burned. How the teacher was in horrible shape herself, but was carrying one of the students on her back. How she kept encouraging the girls. And how the flames swept over them as they were trying to escape.

The witness just barely escaped herself. "There was nothing I could do. Please understand . . . I hope you can understand," she said, sobbing.

"It wasn't just her. There was nothing anyone could do."

Kozo imagined the girls helplessly curling up, enveloped in flames. And the one in the center holding them all tight with one on her back was Sumi. "But if there was a witness, then that last girl—the one the family didn't accept—must have been Aunt Sumiko's student, too, right?" he asked, and his grandfather nodded but was silent for a moment. He seemed to be trying to decide if it was all right to say what he was about to say.

"I thought the same thing. So I went back one more time. I figured if she was in a stable place, I could tell her about the witness and give her the bones. I thought maybe that would give her some closure."

But when he arrived at the house, it was all closed up. Most buildings that were deemed unsafe to live in were abandoned like that.

Had that mother gone somewhere else? Or had something happened to her? Kozo's grandfather went to the house next door to ask.

"She went into the water." The young woman who'd answered reluctantly pointed to the bridge over the river out back. "A firefighter found her floating downstream."

When she saw he was rendered speechless, she said, "Wait just a moment, please," went into the house, and came back with an older woman who must have been her mother or mother-in-law. The story she told was hard to hear.

The girl, Sumi's student, was named Toshiko Kawamoto. Her father had been an officer in the navy, but he had died in battle two years prior. After that, it was just the girl, who looked just like him, and her mother living together in a close bond.

"She was a strong woman dedicated to raising her daughter even after losing her husband. She was so happy when Toshiko got into R Girls' School. She even managed to scrape together the ingredients for red bean rice somehow. She brought some over to share. We were only just celebrating together. . . ." The woman nodded and added, "Toshiko was such a clever girl, and so kind."

The mother's despair when she lost the daughter she cherished was so deep that after searching so hard, her mental state deteriorated, and she threw herself into the river at the end of autumn.

"Her face was pale and she kept glancing toward the water. She said she'd heard that lots of people had died in the river."

The older woman had tears in her eyes.

"If only we could have looked out for her a bit more."

The younger woman rubbed the older woman's back.

"My family all died, too. I'm lucky to have this girl with me."

After thinking for a moment, Kozo's grandfather had them give him the name of the family's temple. As luck would have it, they were the next plot over at the same place.

So from there, he took the bones to the temple. The gentle priest listened to his story in silence and then accepted the bones.

"I asked if we should put them in our family grave, but the priest said that if you know for sure the bones belonged to someone else, that wasn't allowed."

"So is she buried with her mother . . . ?"

"I wonder. For better or worse, the priest said he would accept the remains and pray for the dead. I think he accepted the weight of my burden and shouldered it with the Buddha."

No one could have known which of the six children's bones were theirs. So Kozo's grandfather was sure all the families were nervous about accepting.

"Although some parents said that if God or Buddha really existed, nothing this horrible would have happened, so they weren't worried about any punishment."

Kozo's grandfather fell silent for a little while again, but then said, as if to tell himself, "Really, she's fortunate that there were even bones to enshrine."

Kozo remembered the story he'd heard from Nozomi

about the comb—the comb Mr. Yoshioka had given to Satoko. They hadn't found anything else, so they buried the comb.

"There were all sorts of other things people buried when no bones were found. . . ."

When Kozo told the story about the comb, tears wavered in his grandfather's eyes.

11

Each Person's Story

"*I* think I finally get it," Kozo told Shun and Nozomi. "Whenever anyone in my family talked about Sumi, I thought it was weird because it always sounded like they were talking about someone living, but I think I understand why now."

Kozo felt that in some corner of their minds, his grandfather and the others were still waiting for Sumi to come home—even if they knew logically that she wouldn't.

"It seems like they're still waiting for her to come back."

"Maybe your family has regrets the same way Mr.

Yoshioka and Mrs. Sudo do. And things they wanted to say to her."

"Things they wanted to say?"

"Mr. Yoshioka probably wanted to say *Sorry.* That and *See you tomorrow.*"

"And Mrs. Sudo?"

"*See you later. Come straight home.* Or maybe *I'm not mad anymore.*"

"I think my grandpa and everyone saw Sumi off in a good mood like always . . . she just didn't come back like always." Kozo thought carefully as he spoke. "Maybe they aren't sure the bones were Sumi's . . . and the same about her students'."

"The art club's theme for the cultural festival is Hiroshima, and we're accepting submissions from anyone. What if you drew this story, Kozo?"

People burned so badly in the raging flames that they were unidentifiable. Six little skulls around one larger skull. The scene was horrific, to be sure, but for some reason when Nozomi heard Sumi's story she thought of a mama bird sheltering baby birds or a mama cat carrying her kittens by the scruff of their necks.

"I think it would be a really emotional piece."

"But I can't draw."

"Still . . . don't you want other people to know the story?"

"I do. . . . My grandpa said someone wrote a tanka about a similar scene."

Kozo wrote the poem he'd memorized into Nozomi's notebook bit by bit.

The bigger bones must be a teacher's; small skulls gathered around

"It's by Shinoe Shoda."

"So does that mean there were other adults who sheltered kids, too?"

The three of them stared at the poem.

"I thought one of you two could paint it," said Kozo.

"I don't have the time. I'm putting a lot of effort into the piece based on Mrs. Sudo's story, and I have that huge canvas, too."

Kozo's face fell.

"Plus, it's your aunt's story. You should be the one to do it. Ask your family for more details."

"I guess I could have my grandfather help me. . . ."

"Your whole family could work on it. I heard someone else asked the same thing—if they could do a piece with their mom."

But Kozo still didn't seem very confident, and he turned to Nozomi. "You're done with yours already, aren't you?"

"But I think I'm going to do one more. . . ."

That left Kozo upset. He probably never looked so miserable on the baseball diamond.

"You gotta step up," Shun said, urging him, and Kozo finally nodded.

It was true that Nozomi had one more picture she wanted to paint. She had finished the story of Mr. Yoshioka and Satoko faster than she could have guessed. She had never met Satoko, but the woman even appeared in her dreams. She didn't have to think about the composition; while Mr. Yoshioka was gone she had her easel set up in the empty space by the window looking out at the school's gate.

I think Mr. Yoshioka will say that he can tell there's a lot of heart in this piece.

Shun stopped by often to look at her work, but while he'd usually have lots of harsh comments for her, this time he was quiet. All he said was "I'll have to tell my sister to come see it."

On her way home after splitting with Kozo and Shun, Nozomi was thinking about the other painting she wanted to do. Before she'd heard about Satoko, she had been planning on painting the lantern floating ceremony.

That summer, her mother had released a white lantern again. She wanted to finally ask who it was for, but recalling her mother crying alone on the night of the ceremony the previous year, she couldn't bring herself to ask anything.

Why did it seem like the white lantern had stood out from all the others? Maybe because it didn't have a name on it?

Along with that image, there was an image that kept coming to mind: the eyes of that elderly woman staring at her, the tears that had overflowed as she asked her mother's age. . . . There had to be some story Nozomi didn't know.

She remembered the story Kozo had told them, about people who had died. Girls her own age. The young teacher who had died holding those students close. Families left behind. The mother who cast herself into the river.

Unidentifiable bones. Dead whose names were unknown. And the people who can't forget those who never came home.

Nozomi decided that when she reached her house, she would try to see what it was her mother had been looking at that night.

In the drawer of the decorative rosewood cabinet, there were several notebooks. They all had beautiful covers of washi or wrapping paper.

She recognized the top one, wrapped in colorful paper. It was a record of congratulations or condolences received. And that's what it said in her mother's soft handwriting. She said she had started keeping it because Grandma had told her to not forget the thought or to send a thank-you. But it wasn't a notebook her mother had been looking at that night. It was smaller and thinner.

Of the other two notebooks, one was an address book. The other was wrapped in blue paper and didn't have anything written on the cover. When she shook them both, something fluttered out of the blue one.

It was an old photograph wrapped in paper.

Two people were in it, a young man and a young woman. The woman was her mother—her mother at a young age. Her hair was tied back in pigtails and she wore a white blouse with a round collar and a skirt.

The one difference was that, just like her mother had said, her cheeks were much rounder—just like Nozomi's were now. If it weren't so old and in black-and-white, she might have been able to pass it off as a picture of herself.

I really do look like my mom. The moment she thought that, she remembered the old woman from that night.

That strange expression. Her tears.

Was she looking for my mom? My mom, only as a kid? Who was that lady?

Nozomi's daydream—or maybe she had to call it a fantasy—from that time came back to her.

Is she my mom's real mom? Is my mom the daughter that woman lost when the bomb fell?

Nozomi tried to recall exactly what the old woman had said to her. She copied the way her grandma looked when she was looking for something and sat quietly with her eyes squeezed shut and her hands pressed to her temples, trying to remember that night.

The first question was "How old are you?" Then she asked, "Do you have an elder sister?"

So she had been looking for someone a bit older than me. Maybe fifteen or sixteen?

But that didn't add up. The bomb was dropped in 1945, twenty-five years ago. A girl who was fifteen or sixteen last year wouldn't have been born yet. *So then she wasn't looking for someone lost during the bombing?*

What did she say to me next? "How old is your mother?" I think.

When she had answered "forty-two," the woman's face had twitched, but she seemed to think the answer made sense. The lady must have been looking for Nozomi's mother—a girl who had been a little older than Nozomi at the time, in her mid-teens.

Nozomi started to feel more and more certain about her sleuthing.

But what for? Why was she looking for her? Because she's her daughter?

When Nozomi told her mother about the old woman, she had seemed surprised. But she didn't say anything.

And then, that same night, when Nozomi woke up, her mother was sitting in the altar room. Only the votive light was on, and something white had stood out from the darkness in her mother's hands.

She had the feeling this little paper package in her hands right now was the item. When she looked closely there were little marks on the paper. Spots like dried tears. Were these the stains of her mother's tears from when she'd hung her head there? *What was she crying about?*

Nozomi looked at the young man in the photograph. He looked two or three years older than her mother. They stood a little apart from each other, seeming shy. But they also seemed happy to be having their picture taken together. You could even say they seemed delighted. . . .

Nozomi gazed intently at the old photo.

Just then, her mother called her. Nozomi returned to herself with a start. She hurriedly put the picture back and shut the little drawer.

That night, she resumed her detective work.

Her mother had married her father at age twenty or twenty-one. She heard they'd had trouble having children, so her mother was just about thirty by the time Nozomi was born.

It was her father's second marriage. The picture of the beautiful woman at the family altar was his first wife, Kumiko. Nozomi's mother always released a lantern for her. Her father had never come to the ceremony. She remembered her grandma saying it was probably too painful for him. "Satoru hates crying in front of people."

Nozomi was the one who said that even the people you think you know, you sometimes don't know so well at all, but the truth of it hit her: she really didn't know much about her mother or father.

Her father lost his beloved wife when the bomb fell. She had heard the story many times from her grandma, but never from him. Maybe it was too hard for him to talk about it, just like how he couldn't come to the lantern floating ceremony.

Maybe Mom was an A-bomb orphan. What if the lady last year was her real mother, but they got separated after the bomb fell and lived apart all these years? What if Gramma took her in and raised her?

She remembered her aunt saying once, when they were visiting her gramma's, "It's such a shame that your mom had to be someone's second wife even though she's so young and pretty. Sure, there weren't many young men left after the war, but she's too good-looking to be someone's follow-up. All that stuff in the past . . ." She seemed like she was going to go on, but Gramma shot her a look that shut her up.

All that stuff in the past . . . What was her aunt going to say? Nozomi remembered how even as a little kid she thought it was strange. Was she trying to imply that Nozomi's mother had married early because she was an adopted child . . . ? Or maybe . . . ?

She had mentioned to her mother that she was painting a picture on the theme of Hiroshima for the culture festival. She felt bad for sneaking a look at the photograph, but she decided she did want to hear her mother's story after all.

12

Girls Side by Side

"There's some stuff I wanted to ask you about the atomic bomb and the lantern floating ceremony . . . ," Nozomi said timidly, and her mother nodded.

The two of them sat on the porch.

"Who do you think the lady was who talked to me that night?" Nozomi cautiously asked the question that had been on her mind all this time. "Do you think maybe she's your real mom?"

Her mother cracked a smile. "That's the kind of wild idea you've had in your head?"

"She was staring so hard at my face! Probably because I

look just like you. I saw the round cheeks you had around my age in that picture." Her tongue slipped, and by the time she thought, *Oops,* it was too late.

"What picture?"

Nozomi resigned herself to admitting that she had opened the drawer and looked at the photograph.

"Oh, you saw that . . . ?" Her mother sighed faintly and then looked Nozomi in the eye. "I think the woman who spoke to you is probably the mother of the man in the photo with me."

Nozomi didn't know what to think anymore. Why would his mother be looking for her mother?

"He was someone I liked a long time ago."

She said it so simply, Nozomi was caught off guard.

Her mother hurried to add, "But he died in the war."

"In the flash?"

Her mother shook her head. "No, not the flash, but the way he died was just as horrible."

Nozomi waited nervously for the story to continue, but her mother spoke not about his horrible death, but about him.

He was from Osaka and studying at Hiroshima

Teachers' College. She had been working at the reception desk of a nearby infirmary, so they met when he came in not feeling well. She was sixteen, and he was nineteen. His name was Shinji Hotta.

He was the kind of person who was either reading a book or lost in thought, and he always forgot something: the medicine he had only just been prescribed, his scarf, his old wallet. So she always chased him down.

One day he forgot a book. It was a pocket paperback edition of *The Notebooks of Malte Laurids Brigge.* By the time she realized it and went looking for him, Hotta was already gone, so she held on to the book.

She loved to read, so that night she started reading it. There were all sorts of notes and underlined passages. She didn't finish it that night, so when Shinji returned the next day to retrieve it, she asked if she could borrow it. He beamed and agreed to lend it to her.

After that, he started dropping by the infirmary even when he wasn't sick. He brought her all sorts of books. In those times, there weren't all that many books at the bookstores, and even fewer of the kind she would want to read, so she was very happy.

And the two grew close discussing the books they had read. When they realized that the parts they found interesting or heartrending were scarily similar, Shinji said, "Do you know the term 'soul mate'? Maybe we were connected in a past life." Nozomi's mother cheerfully related how excited she was to hear that—until he disappointed her by continuing, "Maybe we were siblings? Or parent and child?"

He was a bit dense in that sense, but as they read more books together, they grew completely comfortable with each other.

The doctor at the clinic took the photograph of them. He wanted to test out his new imported camera, and he gave them each a copy. But Nozomi's mother's copy burned.

"Then where did the one you have in the drawer come from?"

The doctor from the clinic was a very methodical man, so he had sorted all his pictures, put them in albums, and evacuated them to his house in the countryside. Then he shared them with people who'd lost everything in the fires caused by the bomb. That was how she had this one picture of Shinji.

When Shinji went to war, he took the picture in his copy of *The Notebooks of Malte Laurids Brigge.*

"If his things were returned to his mother, she must have seen the photo."

"So that's how she knew what you looked like. . . ." That made sense to Nozomi.

"I loved Shinji very much," her mother admitted.

"Dad'll be mad at you."

"He already knows." She laughed a bit. "He said, 'That's fine, so please marry me.'"

"So that's why you became someone's second wife even though you were still so young and pretty."

"Where did you hear that?"

When Nozomi said her aunt had said it, her mother laughed, but then grew serious again and said, "Honestly, I thought that since he had lost someone precious to him, he would forgive me if I had someone I could never forget."

Her mother was talking about Kumiko, Nozomi's father's first wife. The picture of the beautiful woman was on the family altar.

Kumiko was a delicate, petite woman. Nozomi's father

had always protected and cared for her—apparently to the point that his two little sisters, who loved him terribly, got jealous.

When he returned from the war and found out that Kumiko and his little sisters were gone, and heard about the circumstances of their deaths, he broke down in tears. "If only I had been here . . ." Nozomi had heard that story from her grandma, and she remembered being shocked by the idea of her father sobbing.

"Where did Shinji die?"

"At sea. The one consolation is that we're connected by Hiroshima's rivers." Her mother's voice broke. "It was right before the war ended. . . ."

Just as she trailed off, the phone rang. She looked relieved for some reason and stood up to get it.

"I'll tell you another time. . . . Sometime, okay?"

After a short conversation on the phone, she turned back to Nozomi. "I'll be back. I'm going to pick up your grandma."

Her grandma had gone to the hospital, but as she was about to leave, she'd felt ill, so she was getting an IV.

Nozomi saw her mother off, locked the door, and went to her room.

The story she'd heard from her mother was something she had never imagined. That elderly woman wasn't her mother's real mom. Her mother had been in love with someone. But he died in the war.

A death just as horrible . . . at sea?

The other lantern her mother always released had to be for him. And someone who was maybe Shinji Hotta's mother had come to the lantern floating ceremony last year. Had she come from Osaka?

Shinji's mother must have committed that photograph to memory and then spoken to Nozomi because she looked so similar. And then when she found out she was only twelve, she asked if she had an elder sister. And after she asked, it must have hit her that it had been twenty-five years since the war ended. The girl in the photo wasn't a teenager anymore—she would have been about the age of Nozomi's mother. And that must be why she had asked, "How old is your mother?"

Was she happy to catch sight of Nozomi? To find out that the girl in the picture next to her son had grown up and had a daughter who looked just like her? Or did she think it was horrible of her to have married someone else?

After mulling it over, Nozomi called her mother's mother—Gramma—and asked if she could go visit.

That day, her gramma showed her a letter Nozomi never would have guessed existed. On the back of the envelope was an address in Osaka and the name Michiko Hotta. It was addressed to "The Mother of Miss Yuriko Kizaki."

"That letter came three years after the war ended. It was just as Yuriko was about to get married. I thought hard on it but decided not to show it to her."

The letter was first an apology for writing so suddenly. It went on to say that she was Shinji Hotta's mother, and that there had been a letter for Yuriko among Shinji's belongings, but that she would leave it up to her mother as to whether to give it to her. She would send it over if she liked. Lastly, she said she wasn't sure what their family's circumstances were and that the letter could be discarded and forgotten if it was a bother.

"Yuriko had finally sorted out her emotions well enough to get married, so I wasn't sure if I should stir them up again. . . ."

Nozomi's gramma carefully folded up the letter.

"And I thought Mrs. Hotta must have had that sort of thing in mind, since she addressed it to me. She wrote such a considerate letter that I was sure she would understand." She sighed. "I fretted over it before making the decision, but it was a painful secret to keep."

When Nozomi told her what had happened the previous summer, tears formed in her gramma's eyes.

"She came all the way to Hiroshima, did she? For twenty-five years, she couldn't forget the girl in the picture with her son. . . ."

Nozomi was silent, unsure what she could say, but as the tears trickled down her gramma's cheeks, she finally said, "Do you think I could write a letter? To tell her that I'm going to paint the lantern floating ceremony. And so that she knows the girl she talked to that time was Yuriko Kizaki's daughter. And I'll tell her why you didn't reply. So please don't cry anymore, Gramma."

Her gramma wiped her tears away with her sleeve and nodded.

That night, Nozomi wrote a letter to Mrs. Hotta. She made sure to include the apology her gramma asked her to add, and she sent it from the Kizaki family to make it easy to understand. The answer came immediately.

13

The Reply from Mrs. Michiko Hotta

This may sound inconsiderate, but the first time I saw the lantern floating ceremony, I thought, What a beautiful memorial service.

Once the green and red paper lanterns were lit, it was almost as if they'd been given life, their glow was so otherworldly.

They formed little groups as they flowed quietly down the river. Like souls departing on a journey.

I remember the faces of the praying people. No one moved; they were like stone statues.

A tiny child who knew nothing of that day crouched next to their grandmother, pressed their palms together, and then helped release a lantern.

Children who came boisterously running down the bank hung their heads instinctively, struck by the solemnity of the ceremony.

And all together, we saw the lanterns off in silence. We watched as the lanterns gleamed, creating a glowing path as they bobbed along with their shadows cast on the water, down toward the dark sea.

The beauty of that scene moved me so.

During last year's Bon holiday, I went to the memorial in Tokuyama for the first time. After the twenty-fifth anniversary ceremony ended, I stood gazing out at the sea where my son had gone for so long that I missed my train back to Osaka.

I needed a place to stay for the night. Without thinking too hard, I ended up in Hiroshima. My son had written to me that during his short life, he had an especially fun time in that town. But the Hiroshima my son enjoyed must have been completely obliterated by the bomb.

I had never been, so I wondered how today's Hiroshima would strike me. I knew that the old teachers' college had been turned into a university, so I thought I could at least see where my boy studied.

I got a room at a small inn for businesspeople near the station. When I was chatting with the manager at the front desk, he told me that the lantern floating ceremony was that night.

It happened as I was looking around at the people watching the lanterns. I saw the profile of a girl that startled me. I couldn't believe my eyes. The girl from the picture of my son was there praying to see off the lanterns. Was my son's soul showing me a vision? I was shocked.

The girl looked up and smiled at someone. It was definitely the girl who'd smiled so bashfully in that photo.

Without thinking, I descended to the river's edge. I pushed through the crowd until I was next to the girl.

Up close, she seemed a little younger than the girl in the photo. She turned to look at me, probably because I was staring at her so hard.

I couldn't help but ask, "How old are you?" When she said she was twelve, I knew the girl in the photo wasn't that young, so I asked, "Do you have an elder

*sister?" But even as I asked, I realized that it had
already been twenty-five years.*

*As expected, you didn't have an elder sister. So
perhaps you were the daughter of the girl in the
photograph. It even said "Yuriko Kizaki, 17 years
old" on the back of the picture. If she'd survived
the bomb, she would have been in her early forties.
When I heard how old your mother was, I realized
I was probably right.*

*I felt bad for frightening you. I wasn't sure what
to do, so I got nervous and ran away.*

*I can't express how happy I am to receive this
unexpected letter from you.*

*If I were your grandmother, I probably wouldn't
have told your mother about my letter, either. Please
tell her not to worry about it. She can pretend it
never happened.*

*My son Shinji was sent with other students to
war and died in a special weapon called a* kaiten
*when he crashed it into an enemy ship. Apparently
it happened just three days before the war ended.
He was only twenty years old.*

Have you heard the word "kaiten" before? They were tiny submarines, less than a meter in diameter. They filled them with explosives and used them to attack enemy ships.

But it wasn't just any attack. You've probably heard about the tokkō, *the special attacks. They made live humans into bombs—there is no more horrible way to send people to their deaths.*

I'm sure young people today can't believe that someone would follow an order like that and ram themselves into an enemy ship. They probably think it's an absurd, pointless death.

In Shinji's will, he wrote that he was giving his life to save the people on the home front. He was a sensible boy, so I'm sure he understood how meaningless those special weapons were. But I think that in light of how close we were to losing, when he thought of the people he left behind, he figured that it was the only option available to him—he must have forced himself to believe that everyone important to him would be saved through his death. He didn't complain about anything in his letters, but I'm sure he had regrets.

When I learned that during that short, sad life, Shinji was able to date this girl, Yuriko, I was delighted with all my heart.

The photo of them was inside a slim paperback volume among his personal items I received. It was his favorite book, The Notebooks of Malte Laurids Brigge. I'm sure the young lady in that photo was the person he loved most of all.

Shinji spent all his time studying, but he looked so happy in that picture. It seemed like he wanted to look serious, but couldn't help but smile. It was the same way he smiled when something good happened at school when he was little and he would race home to tell me about it. Trying to compose himself, but blushing a bit. If he had lived and come home, I'm sure he would have told me all about Yuriko.

The letter I told your grandmother about was also in with Shinji's belongings. It wasn't sealed, and he left a note that said, "Mother, please read this and pass it on when the time seems right." He must not have known quite how to handle it, either. But I could never find the right time. When I finally wrote to your grandmother three years after the war *ended, it was because I couldn't even sort out my own feelings.*

I imagine the reason your grandmother didn't pass my letter on to Yuriko was similar.

And the other reason I addressed it to her mother and not her was because I didn't know how Yuriko was doing.

I was worried that there might have been damage from the bomb, but luckily my letter wasn't returned, so I knew it had been delivered. And I figured the reason there was no reply was that her mother had made the decision she felt was best.

What Shinji wanted more than anything was for Yuriko to be happy, so I think it worked out fine. And when I saw you, I was even surer of that.

You really are the spitting image of her, though. I wondered if my eyes were playing tricks on me. Whenever I remembered your face, I thought that maybe I had just spent so long looking out at my son's resting place in the sea off Tokuyama that my eyes and my mind were confused, so I had just seen whatever phantom I had wanted to see.

But some days I wondered if my hunch was right and even considered writing another letter, but I gave up, thinking I mustn't.

If my hunch was right and my son had arranged our meeting, then it meant that Yuriko was blessed with a child and was living a happy life. That was enough for me, so I was so thrilled and grateful to receive your letter.

The fact that among those beautiful floating lanterns was a white one for Shinji, and that Yuriko and her daughter have been welcoming and sending off his soul every year will give me strength to live out the rest of my days until my husband and Shinji come to take me back with them.

That miserable war robbed Shinji of his future and robbed me and Yuriko of Shinji. But young souls like you and your little brother get to see and live in the world Shinji and the others like him are missing out on. That thought alone warms my heart.

May the world your generation lives in be peaceful—I hope with all my heart. May there never be foolish ideologies that bind free minds lurking *there. May you grow up healthy and live out your full life.*

Though from a distance, I pray from the bottom of my heart for good fortune for you and your family.

Michiko Hotta

The girl in the picture next to the boy who died in battle will someday be a mother.

Hitomi Koyama

14

Innocent People

When Nozimi's gramma finished reading the letter from Mrs. Hotta, she sat there quietly for a little while, but then she abruptly stood up and went to get the other letter, the one that had arrived over twenty years ago.

"Let's give both letters to Yuriko."

She said she had been thinking about it ever since talking to Nozomi.

"If she talked to you about Shinji . . . maybe that means she's in a place now where she can talk about what happened twenty-five years ago. If that's the case, then the rest should be up to her to decide."

She was referring to the letter Shinji had left behind.

Nozomi set the new letter gently on top of the yellowed envelope. In her mind, the girl in the photo and her mother overlapped and became one.

Around the same time Nozomi received the letter from Mrs. Hotta, Shun got a letter from Mr. Yoshioka.

After politely thanking them for the visit, their teacher wrote that he had something he absolutely needed to tell them. After reading the letter several times, Shun stared at his nearly finished canvas. He decided to add a few things.

Then he called Nozomi and Kozo about passing on their teacher's message. They agreed to meet after art club the next day.

Have you ever heard the words "innocent people"?

World War II is said to be our first war that involved "innocent people" and ended with so many victims.

There's no such thing as a "correct" war, but there is at least one rule that needs to be followed, and that is to not involve women, children, or the elderly—ordinary citizens who've done nothing wrong. "Innocent people" refers to those citizens who did nothing wrong. You could also call them "noncombatants."

In Hiroshima's case, the entire city burned, and a dreadful number of citizens were victims. You kids have been taught this over and over since elementary school, right? We still don't know the exact number of casualties, but in one instant, more than 70,000 died, and by the end of the year, the total number is said to have reached 140,000.

I'm supposed to be your teacher, so I'm extremely ashamed to admit this, but since the morning of August 6, I've only been thinking about the Hiroshima that vanished, the people who never came back, and myself. I don't know what to do with the anger I've been holding on to, the anger about the fact that someone I love was taken from me.

But Hiroshima wasn't the only place where innocent people were victims. All major cities were firebombed over and over. It was terrible. There were a hundred thousand victims in the firebombing of Tokyo. In the Battle of Okinawa, many civilians, including students, were brutally killed.

And Japan wasn't the only country where

innocent people were victims. For example, in Leningrad, Russia, citizens got caught up in a siege and nine hundred thousand people starved to death. In Italy and Poland, villagers were shut up in churches and burned to death—entire towns were razed. In other Asian countries, including China, countless citizens who did nothing wrong were made victims. I think you've studied about how the Jewish people were persecuted. They were innocent people, too. There are a staggering number of nameless, blameless, innocent people of the world who became victims of this war.

And yet all I could do was grieve for my own loss. Nearly a quarter century after the war ended, I was still filled with self-pity. It was only when I got sick that I could finally step back and take a look at myself from the outside.

We Japanese people, whether we like it or not, became aggressors in that miserable war. We also became victims. Both our crimes and our wounds are vast and profound. How on earth will we be able to make up for these crimes, to heal these wounds? These are things we'll have to ask ourselves as long as we live.

As one answer, scholars of World War II and especially the Holocaust continue to tell us, "Thou shalt not be a victim, thou shalt not be a perpetrator, but, above all, thou shalt not be a bystander."

Finally, I realized that I was deployed as a soldier and became a perpetrator, I encountered the bomb and became a victim, and these twenty-five years since the war ended, I've been nothing but a bystander.

Luckily, you kids aren't perpetrators or victims yet. If there's anything someone like me can say, it's that—and I can only say it in self-admonition— I want for you to live your lives without becoming either. And never become a bystander—I want you to tell people about what happened during the war, what happened in Hiroshima.

I can imagine you, Shun and Nozomi, having read this far, thinking, But will making one little story into a picture really be able to express a problem so huge?

This world is made up of little stories. Those modest daily lives, those lives that may seem insignificant, they give the world shape—that's what I believe. Don't you think that presenting small stories in detail is precisely the most certain way to depict huge things?

I'm really looking forward to seeing all of your art at the culture festival.

"Innocent people . . ."

"That means pretty much everyone in Hiroshima that day. Ordinary citizens, noncombatants . . ."

"Satoko, Mrs. Sudo, Kenji, Sumi and her students . . ."

"But this story about the nine hundred thousand people in Leningrad is awful. Did you know about that?"

"Not at all. I didn't know about Italy or China, either."

"Do you know about the American soldiers who were in Hiroshima that day?"

Nozomi and Kozo cocked their heads.

Shun told them about the American soldiers who were being held prisoner in Hiroshima the day the bomb dropped. Even those who survived were reportedly dragged out and killed.

"By who?"

"Japanese people who lost their families in the flash."

"I read about that before. In a survivor's testimony; she said that people who had been attacked in such a brutal way couldn't help but take their anger out on any American they saw, but that it was still inhuman. She said she felt like a participant in the crime because she didn't stop them, but she understood their anger after their families were killed so cruelly, so she couldn't say anything."

"Right, my grandpa says that one horrible act causes another, and that repetition is how war never ends."

"A handout from our social studies teacher said the same thing. It was a news story from another country. A woman soldier was asked what the point of terrorist attacks was, and she said, 'My husband and children were killed in the war. I have no hope anymore. I can die anytime.'"

"There was a picture, too, right . . . ?"

"Yes, I thought the woman's eyes looked familiar . . . and I realized they were like Mrs. Sudo's eyes."

Nozomi and Kozo remembered how Mrs. Sudo had lost her husband and child, too.

"For people in that situation to go on living, they need some kind of help or reason, I guess."

"For Mrs. Sudo, maybe that was Koyama's poems and Grandma's sushi rolls."

"Food is really important," Kozo commented passionately. "When you feel down and you eat something bad, you feel even worse."

He seemed to be speaking from personal experience, so Shun and Nozomi couldn't help but laugh, but Nozomi continued with a straight face. "And one of the third years was saying that the first subjects deemed unnecessary when the war started were art and music. And did you hear about how a lot of books were banned?"

Shun and Kozo nodded.

"I remember hearing about that. Like, 'Poems are for the weak, so you mustn't read them.' Or you could just be reading any book about philosophy or thought and get hauled in by the special police as a Communist."

Nozomi recalled the line at the end of Mrs. Hotta's letter about "foolish ideologies that bind free minds" and knew that's what she was talking about.

"But actually, pictures and songs, things like that . . . are what might save us the most."

"That's it, isn't it? I don't know much about tanka, but I'll never forget that poem Mrs. Sudo copied into my notebook."

"Or the one about the bones."

Those poems contained the "little stories" Mr. Yoshioka talked about, and they were filled with an intense sadness. They connected the heart of the reader to the heart of the writer so they could share the deep pain and sorrow. *Sharing those feelings can encourage or save people,* thought Nozomi as she recalled the tanka included at the end of Mrs. Hotta's letter. But the feelings inside her were too big to say aloud.

With a little sigh, Shun said, "And pictures, too! I hope someday I can paint an unforgettable picture. . . ."

Nozomi quietly nodded.

15

Hiroshima: Then and Now

The culture festival exhibition collected not only art club members' works, but submissions from the entire school. Nozomi and Shun's theme, "Hiroshima: Then and Now," resonated more than they expected.

Immediately opposite the entrance to the gallery hung the big photograph—of the once brilliant Industrial Promotion Hall and the bright faces of the people of Hiroshima looking up at it.

On the day of the culture festival, someone completely unexpected showed up: Mr. Yoshioka.

Everyone cheered and rushed over to him.

"Mr. Yoshioka, are you out of the hospital?"

"When are you coming back to school?"

"You look so tan. Were you really sick?"

After the initial fuss, Mr. Yoshioka nodded and explained, "I'm resting up till the end of the year. But soon I'll be able to get treatment at home. Today I got special permission to come out." He turned to look at the exhibition. "This is great. You all worked really hard."

Then he walked around to take a careful look at each piece.

All different Hiroshimas were depicted—relatives or neighbors they had never met, things about that day kids had heard from their parents or grandparents. Most of the artwork came with a short statement or explanation.

Each student had found his or her own way to express the pain and sadness deep in the hearts of the people who had inspired their work, as well as the joy and optimism before the bomb fell.

Every piece seemed to have more put into it than a simple "skillful" or "crude" could describe, just like the pictures drawn by A-bomb survivors on display at the Peace Memorial Museum.

In the middle of the section for general submissions was Kozo's picture. He had used crayons to draw girls sitting on a porch talking.

A young woman with a radiant smile was in the center. There were six little girls sitting shoulder to shoulder in their uniforms. All good friends. In the room behind them the dolls were on display. You couldn't call it a very good drawing; the dolls were bigger than the people. But it was Kozo's picture, and you could practically hear the girls' laughter. Alongside the picture was a poem:

The bigger bones must be a teacher's; small skulls
gathered around

Below the poem was written, "Every year, my grandparents release one yellow lantern and six pink ones. They're for their eldest daughter, who was a teacher at a girls' school, and her students."

Mr. Yoshioka spent a long time looking at Kozo's amateur yet heartfelt piece.

The art club's submissions made up about half of the exhibition, and it wasn't just pictures; projects included a sculpture of a hand with keloids, a collage of a torn skirt and blouse inside a glass case, and an objet d'art made of crushed cans painted black.

Shun had submitted a painting and a sculpture. They were displayed side by side under the title *Morning in Hiroshima: Then and Now.*

The painting depicted the Atomic Bomb Dome. In the upper left corner, there was a small silver airplane. The composition was such that the Motoyasu River reflecting the blue, blue sky seemed to flow toward the viewer, and there was a bridge in the foreground. This was the masterpiece he'd been working on since spring on the huge canvas.

One of the things he'd added to the painting after reading Mr. Yoshioka's letter were the three figures leaning on the bridge's railing and looking up at the sky. One of them had blond hair and chains around his ankles. Shun had depicted morning in both the Hiroshima he knew and Hiroshima of the past at the same time.

The sculpture he had squashed many times before it reached its current shape. A little boy was crouched by a lily-pad pot looking at the viewer with a smile, holding a bowl of water he seemed to have just scooped.

Mr. Yoshioka stopped and stood in silence before these two Hiroshima mornings.

Nozomi had created two paintings. One was of the lantern floating ceremony. A white lantern waited for its turn while other lanterns flowed down the river. Two girls who looked like Nozomi and an elderly woman were gathered around it. The elderly woman held a photograph in one hand, and one of the younger girls hugged a book to her chest. The other girl held a brush and was about to put a name on the lantern.

The title was *The Girl in the Picture*. This piece came with a tanka, too.

> *The girl in the picture next to the boy who died in battle will someday be a mother.*

> Hitomi Koyama

In the other picture, a man waved from a window that looked out on the schoolyard, and a woman below had turned around to wave back at him. The woman had her hair up with a comb in it. There was no statement or explanation with this picture, but its title was *The Moon-Viewing Comb.*

It was the day after the culture festival, the Monday they had off, that Mr. Yoshioka called Nozomi.

"I didn't get to release a lantern this summer, so I was thinking of doing it tonight. . . ."

Before Nozomi could ask him anything, he continued.

"All of your art was so good. Seeing your work, I felt even more strongly that all this time I'd only been thinking of myself, full of self-pity. I was so embarrassed."

Unsure what to say, Nozomi just held on tight to the receiver.

"Maybe I haven't managed to truly grieve. It's like thinking only about Hiroshima and not paying any attention at all to the rest of the world."

Nozomi knew he was talking about the way he had parted with Satoko. But what did he mean by "truly"?

"What do you mean, 'truly' grieve?"

"Accepting the death of your loved ones and seeing them off . . . keeping them in your heart . . ."

Nozomi nodded, though they were talking on the phone. Mr. Yoshioka hadn't managed to do that these twenty-five years. She understood his feelings.

After a brief silence, he spoke again. "I'm going to see them off and keep the memories dear in my heart. Not only the people I lost—I want to remember the question of why such an awful thing happened."

Nozomi remembered what he had written to them in his letter. "You mean, how we should pass on what happened and never forget it?"

"Yes. I want to release a lantern with the prayer that we'll be able to do that." He said he had made a number of lanterns about one-third of the normal size. "I was inspired by the art you all did." He said he had made them smaller than normal since it wasn't the usual season and he didn't want to cause a disturbance. "I made a white one. And I made seven that go together, with one a different color. And I made one with a rabbit and the moon on it."

They were lanterns for Shinji, Sumi and her students, and Satoko.

"Can I go, too?"

"You'll come? Can you tell Shun and Kozo, too? And if anyone else wants to come . . ."

Without even asking her friends first she said, "Everyone will definitely want to come!" Then she asked him a favor: she wanted him to make one more lantern—for Kenji.

So it was that that evening Mr. Yoshioka, Nozomi and her mother, Shun and Mrs. Sudo, and Kozo and his grandparents gathered by the Motoyasu River for an out-of-season lantern floating ceremony.

There was a pleasant October breeze blowing along the riverside, but once the sun set, it got a bit chilly.

Nozomi was worried about Mr. Yoshioka's face being exposed to the cold wind, and her mother must have had the same thought, because she looked around and said, "Maybe we should get something warm to drink."

Mr. Yoshioka declined with a smile, pulled a scrunched-up scarf out of his coat, and wrapped it around his neck.

Everyone took the little lanterns he handed them. Some featured pictures, while others had collages.

Kozo and his grandparents took the seven lanterns. His grandfather wrote "Sumiko" on the yellow one. Kozo and his grandmother wrote the girls' names on the other six: "Toshiko, Kanako, Masako, Yoko, Akiko, Noriko." Each of the six washi lanterns featured an illustration of a Hina Matsuri doll.

Mrs. Sudo received a blue lantern. It had a picture of a healthy boy jumping as he turned to look.

Nozomi's mother's lantern was the only one without a picture, but the white paper flecked with silver made such an impression in the twilight.

When they finished writing the names, everyone went down to the water.

Night had fallen, and the Atomic Bomb Dome on the opposite bank cast a dark shadow on the river's surface.

The riverside was equipped with a floating dock where boats could tie up, and the lanterns were lined up on it as Mr. Yoshioka lit each one.

He lit the white lantern last. A line from Mrs. Hotta's letter came to Nozomi as she watched him work.

"This may sound inconsiderate, but the first time I saw the lantern floating ceremony, I thought, What a beautiful memorial service.

"Once the green and red paper lanterns were lit, it was almost as if they'd been given life, their glow was so otherworldly."

It was just as she had written. The lanterns began to glow from the inside, as if they were alive.

Mr. Yoshioka kneeled down and released Satoko's lantern. Mrs. Sudo, Kozo and his grandparents, and Nozomi and her mother followed.

The lanterns slipped one after another into the dark river.

The blue lantern went spinning playfully after the charming rabbit and moon one.

The little girls' lanterns floated in a circle around Sumiko's, and the white one flowed slowly along, seeming reluctant to part with the flower.

"They flowed quietly down the river. Like souls departing on a journey."

As Mrs. Hotta's words echoed in her mind, Nozomi realized that the lanterns were another sort of *utsushie.*

Mr. Yoshioka had made the lanterns in order to keep the images of the departed in sight and mind so they would never be forgotten.

Epilogue

The ten lanterns cast their light of life on the water, making the reflection of the Atomic Bomb Dome shine. The dome no longer looked like a tragic ruin—it reminded Nozomi of the photograph panel.

Back then, the Industrial Promotion Hall must have looked like one big light. Or like a sparkling merry-go-round.

The lively street lanterns must have flickered as cheerful people bustled merrily by. The gleaming light must have fallen on the river, too, and another Industrial Promotion Hall must have floated there on the surface.

It wasn't only the Industrial Promotion Hall captured in that photograph, that "tracing of light"; it was a snapshot of the calmer life the people of Hiroshima had had during peacetime. When Nozomi realized that, a flood of emotions came over her.

It was like something eternally lost was rising up, wrapped in light.

The light of the lanterns illuminating the dome.

Red, blue, green.

Bands of brilliant light floating down the river.

If something were to appear out of this dreamy glow . . .

Nozomi imagined.

. . . it would be a little boat . . . and in the boat there would be a young woman, a little boy, and a young man in a pure white uniform.

Nozomi envisioned it as if in a dream.

The woman who wanted to wait in the hallway. The little boy who wanted to run back home. The young man who wanted to spend his life with the one he loved.

As she daydreamed, she thought she heard faint laughter in her ear.

The giggling of little girls.

The girls must be on the boat, too. They come tumbling off one after the other, and finally their young teacher disembarks. . . .

Nozomi imagined the girls joining hands and circling around Miss Sumiko. They formed a ring and sparkled.

Mrs. Sudo and the little boy joined the ring, and the light grew brighter.

Satoko appeared, tugging Mr. Yoshioka's hand.

The young man in the white uniform took the hand of a slim girl and joined the ring.

So the ring of light would get even bigger.

The ring of light would get so big it would overlap with the reflections on the river.

"Look!"

Nozomi's daydream ended abruptly when someone shouted. When she gasped and returned to herself, Shun and the others were pointing at the water.

At some point, the lanterns had joined a faster current leading to the ocean.

Everyone stood up as if reluctant to lose sight of them.

The many-colored lanterns huddled together as they receded.

They would float on and on, all the way to the sea.

Like souls . . .

Nozomi looked around. At her mother, Mr. Yoshioka, Kozo and his grandparents. They were all seeing off familiar souls.

All that remained was a lingering glow.

The colorful lights sparkled on the river's surface, creating a ray that reached Nozomi and the others.

A Note from the Author

*I*n Hiroshima, ever since "that day," there have been people waiting for someone. A woman staring at children on the bus . . . Maybe she was looking for someone around the same age. A man chasing down someone who passed by him on the street . . . Perhaps he was searching for his sweetheart.

"Well, my daughter . . . ," an old woman begins. When you listen, it's the story of how her only daughter went out that morning and never returned.

After all, in that one bomb blast, the city was erased, and an unbelievable number of people vanished. For those who lost people close to them so suddenly, August 6 is a day that is past but never over—even today, when the rebuilt city has hidden its scars.

It's impossible to imagine the massive damage caused by a single atomic bomb. Even people who managed to survive August 6 couldn't escape the radiation, and by the end of the year, around 140,000 had died. To this day, there are still people suffering from horrible after-effects, including second-generation survivors.

August 6 isn't long "past," and neither is it only a day to mourn the dead. It's also for remembering the catastrophe brought about by that demonic weapon and renewing our vow to never let something so foolish happen again.

About the
Lantern Floating Ceremony

On August 6, 1945, at 8:15 a.m., an atomic bomb was dropped for the first time, on the city of Hiroshima. The bomb took many lives in an instant, but there were also many people who survived with horrible burns. Lots of them, unable to endure the heat and pain, went into the river and died there.

The lantern floating ceremony is said to have started around 1947 or 1948, when people who lost family or friends began releasing handmade lanterns in remembrance. Usually the lantern bore both the deceased person's name and the name of the person who released it, but in recent years, it has become common to see visitors both domestic and international writing messages of peace.

Thus, during the long history of the ceremony, the lanterns have come to be both a memorial and a peace message.

About the Author

Born in Hiroshima, **SHAW KUZKI** is a second-generation atomic-bomb survivor. She received her MA from Sophia University and is the author of a number of books published in Japan. Shaw Kuzki lives in Kamakura, Japan. *Soul Lanterns* is her first novel translated for US readers.

About the Translator

EMILY BALISTRIERI was born in Wisconsin and currently lives in Tokyo. She has translated many works, including Eiko Kadono's *Kiki's Delivery Service*.